Deck the Halls

LEAH SANDERS

Deck the Halls
by Leah Sanders

This is a work of fiction. Names, places, characters, and events are fictitious in every regard. Any similarities to actual events and persons, living or dead, are purely coincidental. Any trademarks, service marks, product names, or named features are assumed to be the property of their respective owners, and are used only for reference. There is no implied endorsement if any of these terms are used. Except for review purposes, the reproduction of this book in whole or part, electronically or mechanically, constitutes a copyright violation.

*To Wendy—
For the encouragement
and late-night writing sessions
that made this book a thing*

CHAPTER ONE
Deck the Halls with Boughs of Holly

"**I** TOLD YOU, KATE. EVERYTHING NEEDS the *personal* touch," Mrs. Cynthia Hall said sharply as she led the way through the front doors of the luxurious Edelweiss Resort. "This would never have happened if you had given it your personal touch. I've told you thousands of times."

Kate Curtis followed closely, pulling her small case behind her and fighting the urge to roll her eyes at her boss's repetitive mantra, but in her mind she consoled her own bruised ego with the thought, *Or maybe you shouldn't have been so terrible to the steward at baggage check.*

"I don't know, Mother," Mrs. Hall's son, Jake Adams, suggested. "It might have been her personal touch that caused the whole fiasco. Did you see the baggage clerk? He was thoroughly distracted by our Kate." He shoved his way into the doorway alongside Kate and stopped beside her, deliberately brushing up against her before stepping past her into the lobby. "It was her flirting that did it. He didn't hear a word you were saying to him." He smirked back at Kate. "Notice she has *her* luggage."

Kate's stomach roiled.

She had once thought Jake hung the moon. He was tall, traditionally handsome with dark wavy auburn hair and that sexy two-day growth on his face.

Then she got to know him.

When Jake had found her alone in the office late one night, that was all it had taken to realize the guy had the personality of an octopus and just as many arms, and he wasn't used to being told *no*.

It had been a huge mistake. One she wanted to forget.

The fact was, she had requested the time off for just that reason when Mrs. Hall announced her vacation. After all, if her boss was on vacation in Wyoming, she shouldn't need a personal assistant. Mrs. Hall had refused, insisting that having Kate close was necessary in case anything came up that needed a *personal touch.*

Now here she was in the mountains of Wyoming in the dead of winter, at a luxury ski resort.

With the devil.

And his mother.

"Kate!" Mrs. Hall snapped.

"Yes?"

"Check us in!"

"Right away, Mrs. Hall." Kate left the two behind and turned toward the registration desk.

The desk clerk greeted her as she approached. "Welcome to Edelweiss Resort. How may I help you today?" The girl had a Swiss-French accent. Nice touch at a luxury Swiss-style resort, made the upscale clientele forget they're in Wyoming.

"Hello," Kate said, smiling back with her best *personal touch* grin. "We have a reservation for Cynthia Hall. A two-bedroom suite and one single room, I believe."

The clerk turned to her computer and typed the information into the system. Her brow furrowed slightly, and she typed some more. Not a good sign.

"Is anything wrong?" Kate asked. She had the confirmation email on her phone, ready to show it if necessary.

"I see the reservation for Ms. Hall. A two-bedroom suite…" She squinted at her screen. "I do not see the single room." She typed a few more keys and continued to squint.

"I have the confirmation email here." Kate set her phone on the desk so the woman could inspect it and pointed to the number at the top. "The reservation was made six months ago. I called and made it myself."

The clerk looked at her email then back at her screen, tapping a few more keys. "I'm sorry, miss. I see the reservation, but somehow the single room has been removed. I'm very sorry. Let me see what I have available."

Kate cast a glance over her shoulder to where Mrs. Hall and Jake sat waiting. Mrs. Hall was looking at her watch. Jake was checking out the rear view of the woman in tight ski pants who had just walked past.

Such a pig.

"One moment please," the clerk said and disappeared into the room behind her.

Kate released a long, slow breath and waited.

A moment later the clerk returned with what appeared

to be her manager. Also not a good sign.

"Thank you for your patience," she said and nodded at the man with her.

"Hello," he said. "I'm Luca." His accent sounded Swiss-French as well. He was tall and wore a red wool sweater with little white reindeer in a broad stripe across his chest. "I understand there is a problem with your reservation today."

"A problem?" Mrs. Hall chirped, suddenly standing beside Kate. "What kind of problem? Kate, you said you took care of this yourself." Fortunately, Mrs. Hall was keeping her voice down. She did pride herself on being discreet… when the situation called for it.

Here in the lobby of a luxury resort, surrounded by her own kind, the situation called for it.

"It's fine, Mrs. Hall," Kate said. "They have your reservation." She would have gone on to explain the problem, but Mrs. Hall cut her off.

"Then why does he say there's a problem?" She turned to Luca. "What is the problem?"

"There's just a small discrepancy, we are working to fix. Your reservation was to include a two-bedroom suite—"

"Yes. Is there a problem with the suite?" Mrs. Hall interrupted.

"No, madame. The suite is all ready for you," Luca said, smiling again. Then he cleared his throat. "The problem is with the single room reservation."

Mrs. Hall glanced at Kate. "Ah, I see. It's your room, Kate. And how do you propose to fix this issue, um…"

"Luca."

"Yes, Luca. What are you planning to do?"

"As I was just about to tell the young lady, we are quite

full this week, and her room was inadvertently reallocated. I can find another hotel in town if she would like. The Edelweiss will take care of the bill, of course."

Kate nodded and was about to accept the offer. It would mean some space, maybe even a little peace and quiet. Not a bad deal.

"Absolutely not. That is quite impossible, Luca. I can't have her miles away in town when I might need her at any moment. She's absolutely indispensable to me. Find something here. Now. I daresay I can make it worth your while." Mrs. Hall leaned closer at that last part, saying it almost confidentially, like she didn't want anyone to think she was offering him a bribe.

The man shared a look with the desk clerk, and she shrugged almost imperceptibly.

"I have one single room on the lower level. It is where we normally house the staff, but—" he started.

"She'll take it. Thank you, Luca. You are a gem!" Mrs. Hall said, laying her hand on his forearm for a brief instant. "Now, Kate, gather our room keys, and let's get settled in. Jake and I are anxious to hit the slopes this afternoon." Mrs. Hall leaned in momentarily to whisper in Kate's ear. "You see, dear, the *personal touch*. You're welcome."

The desk clerk beckoned to a bellhop who hurried to the counter and snatched up the room keys.

"Will you follow me, madame?" he asked cheerfully.

Mrs. Hall waved at Jake to follow her. Kate grabbed her small case as well.

"Miss?" It was Luca. He reached for her suitcase. "I'll show you to your room."

"Before you start unpacking, Kate, call the airline. Track down the luggage. Then come to our suite. We'll need to discuss our needs for the meantime," Mrs. Hall said over her shoulder as she followed her bell hop in the opposite direction.

Kate blew out another long-suffering breath. She desperately needed a new job.

"Ready?" Luca held out his hand toward the opposite side of the room.

"Do I have a choice?"

Luca's warm laugh seemed to wash over her. It was a nice sound. And not one she heard often.

"Don't worry. The dungeon has its perks," he said and started down the hall toward the staff elevator.

"Is one of them the ability to get permanently lost?" she asked as she followed close on his heels. "Because I'm not gonna lie... I could use the peace and quiet."

Luca pressed the button on the elevator and turned to face Kate, seeming to size her up in a glance. "You say the word, I can make it happen."

"Um..." Kate faltered. "I'm a little afraid to get in the elevator with you now."

A deep crimson flooded Luca's face until he was the color of his festive sweater. "Yes, I heard it as it came out of my mouth," he pointed at his face, "but by that time, it was too late. It sounded so much better in my head."

The chime sounded and the elevator door slid open. Kate hesitated a moment, regarding the man before her.

Luca raised his free hand in surrender. "I promise I'm not dangerous."

It was Kate's turn to laugh. She stepped into the elevator, and Luca followed behind her, carrying her suitcase.

The ride down to the staff level was short, but Luca

kept the conversation going.

"You are on holiday with your mother?"

"My m—? Oh, goodness, no. Mrs. Hall is my boss. She's on vacation; I'm working."

"Ah, I see. That explains your need for peace and quiet. And the gentleman?"

Kate rolled her eyes at the use of the peculiar word to describe Jake.

"Mrs. Hall's son. Though I'm not sure you can legally use the term *gentleman* in reference to him. At least not in the strictest definition of the word."

"Ah, yes. I shall use the term loosely then." Luca smiled.

He had a nice smile.

The doors rolled open, and Luca held them with his hand and gestured to Kate. "After you."

"Thank you." She stepped into the hallway and glanced right and left. It was a tad darker down here. The cedar-paneled walls were bare other than a few dimly lit sconces. No pictures or plants or other decorative touches that she had seen in the lobby.

"It's just down this way. Third door on the left." Luca lifted Kate's suitcase to indicate the direction she should go.

"Is it always so dark down here?"

"We don't spend a lot of time down here while we're on shift, so we conserve where we can."

"Yeah, I guess that makes sense. You probably don't get a lot of actual guests down here."

"As a rule, none."

"Oh." The answer worried Kate. Were they breaking rules for her? "Am I going to get into trouble down here?"

"Not to worry. I have authority to make the call. And the rest of the staff will be notified of your situation. It will be fine."

Kate wasn't so certain, but since she had no choice, there wasn't much she could do at the moment.

Luca unlocked the door to her room and handed her the key card. He stepped inside, laid her suitcase on the luggage stand, and switched on the lights.

"You should have everything you need. Restroom is through there." He pointed at the door to his right. "A kitchenette over here. Closet, television, bed." In turn, he gestured toward each area.

Kate stepped around him and scanned the room. "Cozy."

"Unfortunately, you won't be able to order room service down here." He glanced around the room as if deep in thought, then turned back toward her with his eyebrows raised. "However, if you do need anything, you may contact me directly. I can get you whatever you want." He strode to the desk and pulled out a notepad and pen from the drawer. "Here's my extension. This will ring directly to my cell phone. I'll leave it here on the table for you. Don't hesitate to call. Night or day, I'll take care of it. Yes?"

"Thank you, Luca." Her smile came unforced. If ever there was a living example of the personal touch that Mrs. Hall raved about, this was it. "I'll try my best not to have to use it."

"Nonsense." His easy grin flashed at her again. "You are a guest at the resort. I'm happy when you are happy." He bowed slightly and turned to go. "I'll leave you to your peace and quiet now."

As the door clicked into place behind him, Kate's

phone chirped impatiently. "Yes, Mrs. Hall…" Kate said aloud without even glancing at the notification. She exhaled abruptly and went back to work.

LUCA BURK PULLED THE door closed behind him. During his tenure at the Edelweiss Resort, he had seen many underappreciated personal assistants. But this girl… she was in a league all her own. And he couldn't quite put his finger on it, but somehow he knew she was meant for better things.

Maybe it was the look of inspired exhaustion in her eyes, or maybe it was because she reminded him of someone he had known once. Someone he had been trying hard to forget.

Luca shook off the unwelcome memory and headed back to the elevator. The best thing to do was go back to work, distract himself until the mood passed.

CHAPTER TWO
'Tis the Season to Be Jolly

"THE AIRLINES HAVE LOCATED YOUR LUGGAGE in Hawaii, Mrs. Hall. They should have it here by tomorrow evening."

"Tomorrow evening! That is completely unacceptable! Did you speak to a manager, Kate? Did you talk to him *personally*?"

"Yes, ma'am. *She* was very apologetic and will be sending along some vouchers for dinner and a free flight."

"Coach class, no doubt. Never mind, Kate. I'll talk to the president of the airline myself." Mrs. Hall strode to the window and opened the curtains wide with a flourish. "We have a view of the mountain, at least. That much you did right, Kate."

She had meant it as a compliment, no doubt, but Kate

only heard the insult and fought the urge to roll her eyes. Instead, she broached the next subject quickly to avoid the awkward silence that would only serve to accentuate her lack of response to Mrs. Hall's back-handed compliment.

"What will you need in order to get you through until the luggage arrives, Mrs. Hall?"

Mrs. Hall muttered under breath, an indication that her patience was running thin. It was apparent she thought Kate should already know the answer to her own question.

"Kate… what am I paying you for? Use your imagination, dear. I have nothing but my business attaché and handbag. What do *you* think I will need?" She paused as if she expected Kate to answer the question, but Kate knew better and waited her out.

"For starters, both Jake and I want to ski today. We will need suitable clothing and accoutrements for that activity. Afterward, we will need to change for dinner. Find out what some of the other guests are wearing, and make sure our attire falls in line while surpassing them at the same time." She waved her hand back and forth as she spoke as if it didn't matter what Kate chose, then glanced over her shoulder suddenly. "Aren't you writing this down, dear?"

Kate scrambled for her phone and stylus.

Mrs. Hall sighed and turned back to the window. "Sleepwear, obviously."

At that, Jake cleared his throat. "Speak for yourself, Mother." He raised an eyebrow and replayed his suggestive smirk for only Kate to see, then added, "I sleep in the nude."

"Really, Jake," his mother chided, never looking at him. "Stop teasing poor Kate. She has enough to keep her occupied right now without that thought dancing about in her head."

Kate wished Mrs. Hall hadn't used the word *dancing*. The unfortunate visual was blazoned into her mind's eye, and her stomach turned over again. If she made it through the afternoon without vomiting, it would be a miracle.

"We'll eat breakfast in our rooms, so we won't have to dress for it. But I do intend to spend some time strolling through the village before lunch, so plan accordingly. We might possibly be able to get away without changing for lunch. It is Wyoming, after all. I should think some exceptions can be made considering our circumstances." She slapped her hands on her thighs and spun to face them. "That and some basic toiletries should carry us through."

Kate hesitated, waiting for the list of what Mrs. Hall considered *basic* toiletries.

"Well, off with you, Kate! We want to hit the slopes!"

At that Kate bolted for the door. She didn't wait to be told twice.

THE CONCIERGE WAS HER first stop. He would have a list of contacts Kate could use to acquire what Mrs. Hall needed. Since skiing was the first thing on the agenda, she would address that first.

"May I help you, mademoiselle?" The concierge was a distinguished-looking man, dark-haired with a touch of silver at the temples. He wore a black short-sleeved, double-breasted waistcoat with handstitched lapels, embroidered with tiny white edelweiss flowers. Under that was a white silk shirt and a black ribbon tied in a perfectly-proportioned bow around his collar. The gold bar below his right lapel was engraved with the name *Roald*.

Kate stepped forward to his counter and offered her best business smile. "Yes, I hope you can, Roald." She proceeded to ask him for a list of local contacts she could use to order the necessities for Mrs. Hall.

Since Huckleberry Falls was a resort town that pandered to the rich and famous, it should be possible to request a private fitting in Mrs. Hall's suite for most of the things she wanted.

"Everything okay here?" It was Luca. He stopped next to them as Kate discussed her list with Roald.

"Yes, sir," Roald answered cheerfully. "All in order. The lady has some questions about the local clothing boutiques and ski outfitters."

"Very good." Luca nodded and turned as if he would continue on his way but seemed to think better of it and pivoted to face Kate again. "I was going to drive into town to run a few hotel errands. Perhaps you would like to accompany me? I would be happy to stop at some of the shops in town that suit your needs."

"That would actually be kind of perfect." Since she didn't have a rental car, she was going to have to catch the shuttle, and past that, she'd have to find her way around town on her own.

"Excellent," Luca said and gestured toward the front desk. "We can go out through the back, or if you'd prefer, I can drive around to pick you up in the front."

"The back exit is fine." She nodded a goodbye to Roald and followed Luca through to the office area and the employee entrance. If she hadn't already been rooming in the employee area, she might think it was weird that Luca was leading her through employee-only office spaces, but she was working, after all.

LUCA NAVIGATED THE SUBARU expertly through the streets of Huckleberry Falls, pointing out the different shops as they drove past them. He found an empty space in front of the post office and pulled the car in to park.

"Each year during the holiday season, Huckleberry Falls does what we call Adventfenster." He pointed to the window in the second story of the chocolatier. It was decorated with lights and holly, and a giant numeral three, outlined with Christmas lights. Beside that was a silhouette of the three wisemen riding on camels following the star. "If you look around town, you will see many of the windows have already been unveiled."

"That's so cool! The whole town participates?" Kate asked. She took out her phone and snapped a picture of the display.

"Well, there are only twenty-four days of Advent, so the shops that wish to participate have to enter a lottery that is held in June. The winners design a window for Adventfenster. They have been working on their designs for six months. Some of them are quite exquisite."

Kate loved Luca's accent. She was sure she could listen to him all day. The key would be to keep asking him questions. On the other hand, she really did need to stay on task. Mrs. Hall would be calling her any minute to see what progress she had made. How would that conversation go?

"Kate, we want to go skiing. When might we expect you back with our things?"

"I'm sorry, Mrs. Hall, I've just been seeing the village sights with my personal tour guide. He has an accent that makes my knees weak."

"Oh, in that case, take your time, Kate! I completely understand!"

Yeah, no. It would not go over well.

Still, his accent though…

"There's a ski shop across the street, and a general store down just a couple of blocks." Luca got out of the car, walked to Kate's side, and opened her door. "If you'd like, we can order the skiing equipment and have it delivered right away, then we will have a little extra time to walk through the square to see the other windows and the winter bazaar."

The prospect of a leisurely afternoon stroll through town in present company sounded amazing. If the ski shop could deliver what was needed, Mrs. Hall and her son would be on the slopes for several hours. That would leave Kate with time to collect their other supplies at a more relaxed pace.

"How quickly do you think they can deliver?"

"I know the manager here. I'm fairly certain I can get him to drive it up himself if we play our cards right. Just follow my lead." He held out his hand, gesturing for Kate to go ahead of him.

The bell on the door tinkled as she opened it, and the warmth and the aroma of hot chocolate from inside welcomed her. The shop was decorated in keeping with the Swiss tradition of Huckleberry Falls. Luca stepped in behind her and waved at the guy at the desk.

He was in the middle of a conversation with a customer, but he smiled and nodded to acknowledge them. Promptly, a girl who looked about sixteen approached, smiling.

"Luca! What brings you in today?"

"We are looking for ski gear for some guests at the Edelweiss. They are hoping to ski this afternoon." Luca turned to Kate. "This is an associate of theirs — Ms. Curtis."

"I'm Misty. I can help you find whatever you need."

"I'll just discuss delivery with Thomas," Luca said, tossing this thumb toward the guy at the counter he had waved at when they had come in. "Will you be alright?"

"Yes, thank you." Kate watched him walk away.

"Not a bad view, eh?" Misty said, her voice a whisper.

Kate felt the heat rise in her cheeks. "I suppose not."

Misty raised an eyebrow. "Suppose? What do the guys look like where you come from? Because in Wyoming... *that's* hard to come by, even in a resort town."

Desperate for a subject change, Kate grabbed at the closest ski jacket and held it up for inspection. "Do you have this in pale pink?"

IT HAD TAKEN EVEN less time than Kate imagined it would to select the gear, purchase it, and arrange for delivery. In spite of Misty's propensity toward conversation, they were finished in record time, and after a quick phone call to Mrs. Hall and about an hour in pursuit of the other things on

Mrs. Hall's list, Kate was free to roam the village to her heart's content.

With Luca as her personal tour guide, it was shaping up to be a great afternoon.

They wandered through the village bazaar.

"How long have you been working with Mrs. Hall?"

"About five years. I took the job right out of college."

"Seems like she really depends on you."

"I guess. She definitely keeps me busy."

"Do you get to travel a lot?"

"Surprisingly little. I mean, she does take frequent trips, but they are usually only for a couple days, so I stay behind to keep her office work from piling up. I'm pretty much on the phone with her 24-7 while she's gone. This is the first time she's taken a vacation in I don't know how long. I was actually hoping she wouldn't need me at all and I could get a little time off."

"I take it the request was refused."

"Yep." Kate shrugged. "What ya gonna do?"

Luca pointed to a booth selling hot apple cider. "Want some?"

"That sounds good," Kate said. "So, can I ask you a question?"

"Sure." He cast her a sidelong glance. The look on his face told her he already knew what she was going to ask.

"Why? Why, of all the places on this earth, would you leave Switzerland to work in Wyoming?"

He laughed, and the warmth of it spread through her chilled bones.

"That is the question!" Luca shook his head, and the joy faded from his eyes just a bit.

"I mean, don't you miss it?"

"It will always be my home, yes. I miss it. But—" Luca hesitated as if lost in a memory. "Sometimes you have to move on in order to move on." He laughed again and handed her a cup of steaming hot cider. "Besides… Wyoming isn't so bad. Look around!" He glanced around him at the skyline. "The mountains here are beautiful. The snow, the village, the people… it's as close to home as I could hope for."

"It is beautiful here." Kate took the cup and held it to her lips for a moment, inhaling the sweet aroma.

"You say that like you can't believe it."

"Well, it's hard to believe a place like this exists in Wyoming. I mean, I'm not gonna lie, I've driven through Wyoming a few times. There's literally a sign on the freeway that says *Point of Interest* and it's pointing to a large rock in the median. And that is about as exciting as the trip has ever gotten." She sat on the café chair he held out for her and took a sip of her cider.

"And there's always the danger of becoming hypnotized by the windmills on the side of the freeway, let's not forget."

"Oh, my word! Right? That's so dangerous! See? You know what I'm talking about."

"Yes, I've taken that trip once or twice myself. It was more relaxing than you want driving on the freeway to be."

Kate laughed. "So that really begs the question, doesn't it?"

"Why Wyoming?"

"That should be the state motto."

"I think it is, actually."

Kate sipped at her cider and studied Luca. He seemed so at home here. Not just because he was sitting in a Swiss-style village bazaar sipping hot cider. But he belonged here.

And in that moment, she kind of felt like she did too.

"What about you? Where are you visiting from?" Luca asked, eyeing her over his mug.

"New York."

"Ah! The big city. Have you always lived in New York?"

"Me? No. I'm actually from Idaho."

His eyebrows shot up in surprise, then just as quickly drew together in confusion. "Idaho?"

Kate shrugged. "How would a girl from Idaho end up in New York?" She put what he was probably thinking into words.

Luca set his cup down and leaned forward expectantly.

"I wanted to be in fashion. When you want to work in fashion, you go to New York."

"Do you miss it? Idaho, I mean."

"I suppose I do. Like you said, it will always be home." A twinge of homesickness surged down her spine. It had been a long time since she'd felt that, and she pushed it away. "My life is in New York now."

"I see. Your friends… your boyfriend?"

It was Kate's turn to be surprised. "Boyfriend? …no. I don't have time. My job is pretty demanding." She chewed her lower lip. "Actually, I… I don't have friends there either. I mean, there are people at work that I…" No. That was a lie. She never interacted with anyone outside of the office. In fact, she never interacted with anyone other than Mrs. Hall and her closest associates *inside* the office. Her *life* in New York wasn't much of a life.

Luca was staring at her. Waiting for her to continue.

Waiting for the end of her sentence. When she hesitated, his eyes softened in understanding, and he cast a look over his shoulder.

"I see the pastry booth has brought out fresh *Miroir*. Would you like to try one?"

Kate traced his gaze to the cookie stall. The proprietor was setting a large platter of jam-filled cookies on the table. "I would love that." She swallowed the last of her cider and rose to follow Luca to the cookies.

CHAPTER THREE
Sing We Joyous All Together

WHEN KATE'S PHONE CHIRPED AT HER before the 6:00 A.M. alarm could go off, Kate nearly jumped out of her skin. If she were at home in her own bed, it might not have scared her so badly. She might even have been expecting it. But waking up to it the first morning in a strange room and a strange bed threw her into confusion, and it was several minutes before she remembered where she was.

She grabbed the phone off the nightstand and squinted at the too-bright screen.

5:27.

What the actual heck.

Kate groaned and let the lead in her eyelids coax her back into sleep. Phone still in hand, hanging precariously over the edge of the bed, she lay back on the pillow and snuggled into her fuzzy blanket. A second chirp erupted, jerking her abruptly into consciousness, and she dropped the phone onto the floor with a loud thump.

She leaned over the side of the bed and reached toward the floor, swiping her hand from side to side trying to locate the device. When her fingertip brushed against the rubber casing, she shifted her weight to reach just a little farther. Just as she tightened her grip on the phone, her balance tipped, and she tumbled headfirst out of the bed onto the floor, managing to scrape her head on the corner of the nightstand on the way down.

For a moment, she just lay there in disbelief — a crumpled heap, legs still tangled in the blanket and face pressed into the abrasive carpet fibers, muttering, "What. The. Actual. Heck."

Grudgingly, she clutched at her phone and drew it up to her face to see the notification screen.

Two texts.

From Mrs. Hall.

At 5:30 in the morning.

Oh, how Kate needed a new job.

CSA: YOU HAVE TO GO THE AIRPORT THIS MORNING. OUR LUGGAGE WILL BE THERE AT 9:00.

CSA: ARE YOU UP?

Not cool, Cynthia.

She tapped in her response.

ME: YES, I'M UP.

The irony of the word *up* was not lost on her. Kate rolled onto her back and kicked violently to free her feet from the knot of blankets and sheets.

The reply came immediately with a demanding chirp.

CSA: Then get dressed and get up here. We have to go over the schedule before you leave.

Kate rolled her eyes and let another groan escape her throat. It was 5:30 in the morning… even the sun had better sense than to be up at 5:30 in the morning. She was almost certain that was true even in Wyoming.

ME: I'll be there in fifteen minutes.

CSA: Five.

"It's 5:30 in the morning," Kate said aloud to herself.

CSA: It's 7:30 in New York.

Did she just—? No, there's no way Mrs. Hall could have heard Kate's objections.

She decided to risk it and added, "But we're not in New York, *Cynthia*."

Despite her verbal protest, she pushed herself up from the floor and grabbed her sweats off the chair. If Mrs. Hall wanted her in five minutes, she couldn't be expecting perfection, just punctuality. Sweats, a hoodie, and a messy bun would have to do.

Luckily, at this point in the morning, there wouldn't be too many people in the public areas that might catch her in such disarray. But maybe she would take the employee elevator just to be safe.

Kate slipped her room key and cell into her pocket and headed out the door into the dimly-lit corridor. She glanced up and down the hallway.

All was quiet.

She pulled the door closed behind her and heard the lock snap into place. She moved silently up the hall to the service elevator and mashed the call button.

The door dinged and rolled open; Kate stepped inside and pressed the button for the third floor. The doors began to close but stopped suddenly when a hand thrust in and swatted them back open. Before Kate knew what was happening, Luca joined her in the elevator.

His eyes lit up with recognition when he saw her.

"Good morning, Ms. Curtis. You're up very early today," he said. He tapped the button for the top floor.

Kate thought of her sweats and her messy bun, and she could feel the embarrassment warming her neck and ears. "I… I didn't think anyone would be up and around. Sorry."

"The day starts early for us. But don't worry about it. You're welcome to use the service elevator whenever you wish. Even if it *is* an ungodly hour of the morning." Luca smiled, and once again, his grin warmed her.

Kate was beginning to love Luca's smile.

"Mrs. Hall thinks we should still be operating on New York time," Kate said and rolled her eyes before she realized what she was doing.

"The nerve of some people!" Luca's eyes twinkled with irony as his gaze swept over her and seemed to be assessing her in all her early morning mess.

She brushed a stray curl out of her face and shifted onto her other foot self-consciously, feeling the weight of his stare.

"I really wasn't expecting to see anyone. I kind of took the service elevator for that specific reason. I must look terrible."

"Not at all. In fact, I was just thinking how nice you look."

Kate frowned. "Sure you were."

"Oh, come on. Why would I lie?"

"Oh, I don't know… I'm sure being in the hospitality business would have no impact on your being nice to guests."

"*Touché.* Well, if it helps, it is far too early in the morning to have to think of fake nice things to say."

"That's just the sort of thing I'd expect a flatterer to say at 5:30 in the morning." Kate hid a yawn behind her hand.

Luca chuckled in response. "May I just say, Ms. Curtis, you make early morning duties almost tolerable."

"I was just thinking that same thing about you, Luca." It was out of her mouth before she could stop it. Kate quickly looked away, feeling the burn of embarrassment coloring her ears, which were shamelessly exposed by the hair pulled up into her messy bun.

In that moment, the elevator bell chimed, and the doors slid open to Mrs. Hall's floor.

"Now, *that*, I almost believe," Luca said, and stepped aside to let her exit.

Kate didn't look back until the doors rattled closed behind her. Her reflection in the steel doors met her, and she cringed at the sight. She lifted a hand to straighten her lopsided pile of hair, then swiped at the mascara smeared under her left eye.

"That's just great, Kate. 'I was just thinking how nice you look.'" She mimicked Luca's comment in a deep voice, taking care to get the French accent just right. "Sure I do. That's just great," she muttered to herself.

Her phone chirped impatiently in her pocket.

"Alright, alright! I'm coming!" Kate whisper-yelled into the silence, spun on her heel, and hurried down the hall toward Mrs. Hall's suite.

She knocked on the door and immediately heard the latch click. The door swung open. Mrs. Hall stood there looking gorgeous as ever. Completely made up and put together at 5:30 in the morning, as if she had an important photo shoot.

"Oh, for heaven's sake, Kate, what *are* you wearing?" A frown creased Mrs. Hall's forehead for an instant before she caught herself and smoothed her facial expression again. Mrs. Hall had amazing control over her facial expressions. It was rare that she frowned, and always when it happened, Kate knew that she'd be asked to make an appointment with Mrs. Hall's dermatologist within the week. "Never mind." Mrs. Hall shook her head. "Just come inside. We haven't much time before you will have to leave for the airport."

Kate followed her inside but waited before responding. The airport would surely deliver the luggage to them if they asked. Especially since it was their mistake that caused the problem in the first place. She hoped that Mrs. Hall would think of that solution on her own.

"I spoke with the president of the airline last night. He was able to speed up the return of our things to this morning. It will arrive at nine o'clock. I want you to be there to meet it, so there is no room for error this time."

There it was. The reason Mrs. Hall could not allow the airline to deliver the luggage to them at the resort. Of course. Kate should have known.

The personal touch.

Mrs. Hall sat down on her couch and picked up her phone. "Since you'll be going into the city, I'd like you to handle a few other errands while you're there. I'll text you the list."

"Should I rent a car while I'm there? It might make the trip back a little easier."

"I wouldn't think so, Kate. Just take the train. I don't

want to chance anything happening on the winter roads with our luggage. You don't drive much in New York, and I have heard that the road between here and the city is particularly treacherous this time of year, especially for an unseasoned driver."

Unseasoned? Kate had grown up in Idaho. She'd driven on snowy, treacherous roads many times. She was anything but *unseasoned*. Kate fought the urge to roll her eyes. Instead, she cleared her throat and asked, "So take the shuttle between the train and the airport?"

Mrs. Hall glared at her as if trying to decide if the question was worth answering.

"No, Kate. I want you to walk the three miles dragging our luggage through the ice and snow."

It took a moment for Kate to determine if Mrs. Hall was being serious. It did sound exactly like something Mrs. Hall would ask her to do... minus the dragging of the luggage. That she would want Kate to carry on her head like an African woman balancing a water jug.

Clearly, it was too early in the morning for sarcasm.

"Of course, take the shuttle, Kate." Mrs. Hall shook her head in disgust. Then waved her hand dismissively. "Ask at the front desk for someone to go along with you to help with the luggage. Let them know you'll make it worth their while. I'm sure they have staff for such things. Did you get the list?"

Kate's phone buzzed. She pulled it out of her pocket and saw the notification.

"Yes. I have it."

"Fabulous." Mrs. Hall set her phone on the end table. "Kate—" she squinted as if trying to see some detail on Kate's face. "What is that on your forehead? Is that... Is that blood?"

Kate's hand shot up to her hairline where it still stung. It was wet, and when she pulled away to look, blood stained her fingertips.

"Honestly, Kate. I hope no one saw you skulking through the halls dressed like a vagabond and looking fresh out of a midnight mugging." She stood and offered Kate a tissue. "Now, go get dressed properly and get on the train. I want my luggage."

Kate pressed the tissue to her wound and turned to leave, but Mrs. Hall stopped her.

"Be sure to be back in plenty of time for dinner. I have made arrangements to eat with a few people, and I will need time to get my clothes pressed and ready. Plus, I need you here in case there are any other issues that arise."

Kate moved toward the door.

"I'll call the front desk to get you an escort and some help with the luggage. That way you'll have time to clean up," Mrs. Hall offered.

"Thank you."

By the time Kate got back to her own room, she had the bleeding under control. She pulled out her first aid kit and cleaned up the scratch, then put on a bandage. Staring into the mirror, she took a deep breath and blew it out slowly.

It was a couple hours by train into the city, then another ten minutes on the shuttle to get to the airport. The trains ran every half hour, so she would have to be on the 6:30 train, and it was still fifteen minutes into town from the resort. And yet here she stood, just staring at herself in the mirror…

There really wasn't time to waste, so she quickly went

to the closet and pulled out her black Citizen skinny jeans and vintage black turtleneck. Those, with a scarf and the new Cynthia Skye-Adams long pea coat and her black Prada booties, would do just fine. She ran a brush through her hair and pulled a black wool beanie onto her head. A splash of Dior spray foundation and her Charlotte Tillsbury red lipstick, and she was ready to go.

She grabbed the door handle to leave but suddenly remembered.

She couldn't go into public without her Chanel stud earrings. Mrs. Hall would have a conniption if she knew Kate was stepping out the door without that signature look.

WHEN THE PHONE RANG at the front desk, Luca was standing right next to it going over the day's schedule. The screen identified Cynthia Hall in the Mountain View Suite. Renate was busy with the morning list of arrivals, so he answered it.

"*Bonjour*, Madame Hall. This is Luca. How may I be of service?"

"*Bonjour*, Luca. I hope you'll be able to help me." Her voice had the hint of pout he had heard many times from the female guests. And he could picture that wounded puppy dog look she probably had worn successfully a million times before to get what she wanted. "As you know, the airline lost our luggage yesterday. My assistant Kate will be down there in a moment. She is making a trip into the airport this morning to pick it up. She will need an escort. Someone who can help her with the luggage. Do you have someone available this morning?"

Luca glanced around the office. Normally, he would send Peter on the airport runs, but Peter's wife had gone into labor at two o'clock that morning.

However, Luca did need to go into the city today to purchase necessary supplies for the Christmas ball. So if he sent someone else to escort her, when he had to leave later, it would leave the resort short-handed. It only made sense that Luca should escort her himself. Besides, spending time with Kate Curtis was not a burden by any means.

"We will be happy to escort Ms. Curtis to the airport to retrieve your luggage, madame."

"Excellent! The luggage will arrive promptly at nine o'clock. I have instructed Kate to be there in time to meet it. She will be down directly. Please have your man ready to leave right away."

Luca glanced at the clock on the wall. They would have to leave in the next couple of minutes in order to make the 6:30 train.

"Consider it done, Madame Hall."

"Thank you, Luca." The phone clicked in his ear.

He returned it to its cradle and strode into the office to grab his keys. The image of Kate Curtis in her baggy sweats and dark, messy hair leapt to his mind, and he could feel the hint of a grin playing on his lips.

No. Kate Curtis was not a burden.

Not at all.

"Thanks for doing this. You sure you can spare the time?" Kate asked as she buckled into Luca's Subaru for the second time within a space of twenty-four hours. Not that she was complaining. The amount of attention Luca was paying to her particular needs was amazing. And she had enjoyed the afternoon she had spent with him in the village the day before.

But Luca was a manager at a busy resort.

A totally hot, sexy, Swiss guy with a French accent, manager of a resort that pandered to very important people.

It didn't seem quite right that he would have this much time to devote to just one guest. A guest that was only there because of her very-important employer.

Maybe something else was going on here.

She'd seen it before.

With concierges in other hotels she'd visited with Mrs. Hall.

Exotic guy. Vacationing women. It was the perfect set up for a long string of one-night stands.

The perfect job for a guy like Jake Adams, actually.

It was a wonder she hadn't realized it before.

Suddenly, Kate felt very uncomfortable on her heated leather seat.

"It's no trouble at all," Luca answered. "I have to pick up a few things for the Christmas ball anyway, so I would be making this trip today regardless. I'm just happy to have company."

I bet you are, Kate thought, inching closer to her door. Why had she sat in the front seat?

What a stupid question. Was she going to sit in the back of a Subaru for a fifteen-minute drive into the village and then ignore him for two hours on the train? No. That's ridiculous. She wasn't a desperate socialite hoping to escape her tedious upper crust life and throw caution and her inhibitions to the wind. She was working.

Kate was always working.

That meant no time for exotic men and the romantic interludes that went with them.

She stole a furtive glance at the man in the driver's seat.

Hmm, pity. But no. She wouldn't be one of his conquests. Not this week. Not this lifetime.

Of course, that didn't mean she couldn't enjoy Luca's company. He was easy on the eyes and on the ears. And she had to be there anyway.

Once on the train, Luca and Kate settled in. Luca placed his messenger bag in the overhead bin and asked Kate if she wanted her purse up there. She didn't.

It was still dark outside, and there were very few people on the train that early. A handful of commuters, and a family of locals with a couple of teenagers who looked like they would rather be anywhere else.

"It will likely be full on the way back," Luca whispered as he sat down across from her. "There are always more coming in than going out. Especially at this time of day."

"Do you have to take the train very often?"

"Probably once a week. Sometimes I drive if the roads are decent."

"And how often do you have to escort guests into the city?"

"Me personally? Or the resort in general?"

"Wouldn't they be the same?"

"Peter usually does the escorting. Today just

happened to be my lucky day."

"I see. You drew the short straw, did you?"

"Hardly." He grinned at her and his blue eyes twinkled. "If you want the whole story, Peter is off today. His wife went into labor around 2:00 this morning, so he is with her and his brand-new baby girl at the hospital right now." Luca held up his phone for Kate to see the picture of a man—probably Peter—with a broad, proud smile, holding a tiny bundle of pink. "And since I have to make the trip anyway, I volunteered to take one for the team."

"She's beautiful," Kate said, although she couldn't really see much of the baby herself. It seemed like the thing to say. "Is this their first?"

"She has two older brothers—twins. They are three years old, I think. Frederick and Victor. They are full of energy. I spent Thanksgiving with them."

"Sounds like they have their hands full already." Kate glanced out the window into the pitch-black morning.

"Do you have any siblings?" he asked.

"No. Well, that's not entirely true. I do have a half-brother and sister, but I was raised an only child. They are my father's kids. I lived with my mom." Wow. That was a lot of information to give a complete stranger.

"You don't ever see them?"

"Not really. My father just kind of fell off the face of the planet after he left us, so we have never had any opportunity. I know they exist. That's about it."

Luca studied her. "That's sad. I'm sorry."

Kate shrugged. "It's okay. How about you? Do you have family back in Switzerland?"

He nodded. "My parents, an older brother, and two younger sisters."

"What's that like?"

"Well, living with my two younger sisters was like being in a war zone. They were always fighting about something. I, of course, never did anything to antagonize them and stayed *completely* out of all their arguments." His smirk was almost conspiratorial.

Kate squinted and studied his face. "I get the feeling that is not the whole truth."

"What? I was completely neutral at all times."

"How very… *Swiss* of you," Kate said, offering him an ironic smirk.

He raised an eyebrow, then broke into a smile. "Alright, I confess. I may have been party to *some* secret plots to stir the pot. But only when forced by my older brother. Otherwise, I was entirely innocent."

"I see. Everything was your brother's fault." She chuckled and pulled her coat more tightly around her. There was a bit of a chill in the air still.

Something in his eyes changed at the mention of his brother, and he turned to gaze out the window into the darkness. He didn't respond right away, until just above a breath she heard, "Not everything."

She let the silence stretch out between them.

There was something there. Something about Luca's brother and their history that affected him in a way he didn't seem to be expecting. Maybe it was something so long ago that Luca thought it should be forgotten by now, but somehow this moment had made the memory raw again.

Kate's heart went out to him just a little. Even though she didn't have a relationship with her siblings, she could see that Luca loved his, and that made her want to tell him something to make him feel better. What could she say that would do that?

She had no experience with that kind of thing.

So, she changed the subject.

"Did you say there's going to be a Christmas ball?"

LUCA WASN'T SURE WHERE that had come from. One minute they were making small talk, getting to know each other, and the next he was deep in the mire of days long gone as he drove down the mountain to the village train depot.

He and Liam had been the best of friends growing up, partners in crime. There were two years between them, but Luca remembered being so inseparable that when his older brother had gone to school, he cried the whole day until his brother's return in the afternoon. His mother had called him inconsolable.

It had been that way ever since he could remember. If one was there, the other was soon to follow. But when Amelie came into Luca's life, things changed.

Not that she had ever really been in *his* life.

She had been Liam's girl from Day One, but she had a way of making Luca feel as though she saw only him.

The day Luca realized that wasn't the reality of it was the day he and Liam broke.

And *that* was entirely Luca's fault.

CHAPTER FOUR
See the Blazing Yule Before Us

THE REST OF THE TRIP PASSED pleasantly. Kate could tell the Luca was making an honest effort to push whatever it was that had disturbed him out of his mind and focus on her and what she was saying.

They talked about the village, and he told her the history of Huckleberry Falls. Once again, it was like he was her personal tour guide. Luca really knew a lot about the village and the area surrounding the resort.

Through the window glazed with a halo of frost, they watched the sunrise paint the morning sky with streaks of pink, lavender, and gold.

When the train rattled into the city station, they discussed the plan to get to the airport, claim the luggage, make their other stops, and get back to the train station with all the baggage in tow. Since they both had other errands to run, and the luggage had to be picked up first, the idea of toting all of Mrs. Hall's and Jake's suitcases through the city with them posed a challenge. In spite of Mrs. Hall's previous objections, they would need a car. Just for a couple of hours.

They disembarked and hurried through the freezing morning air for the shelter of the warm station.

"Would you prefer to wait here where it's warm for a few minutes? I can get a car and bring it around to the front," Luca said.

"Sure. You want to just text me when you're out there?"

His eyes darted to hers in surprise. Then he shook his head as if shaking off the shock. "Yes, that will work." Luca pulled his phone out of his pocket and offered it to her. "I guess I'll need your number."

Kate took his phone and tapped in her number.

Her fears earlier that morning had been entirely unfounded, and she felt a little stupid for even entertaining the thought. Luca was not that guy. Not at all. He was exactly what he seemed to be. An honest, sweet, dedicated… super-hot Swiss resort manager guy who was very, *very*, good at his job.

And even though nothing could come of it, she enjoyed spending time with him. Even for just the few days that she would be in Huckleberry Falls.

THE CAR MADE THE rest of the morning run like clockwork. All the missing luggage was accounted for. All the errands on Mrs. Hall's list were checked off. Kate even helped Luca select some of the decorations for the Christmas ball, which Kate had learned, wasn't actually scheduled for Christmas Day. It was to take place the night of the 23rd.

There was a whole festival leading up to it. A pageant, which had kicked off the celebration the day before—Kate was sorry to have missed that part—a parade; a winter carnival with ice skating, games, a Ferris wheel, an ice sculpture display; all culminating in the Christmas ball at the community center where the royal court of the celebration would be announced. It sounded exactly like something Mrs. Hall would enjoy. A place where she could flaunt one of her latest creations and see the gowns of other designers which would, no doubt, be worn by the myriad of well-to-do guests at the resort. Kate wondered if Mrs. Hall knew about the ball.

Luca returned the car while Kate organized all the luggage and packages on one of the carts. They had about ten minutes to wait for the train's arrival. When Luca joined her in the station, there was a dusting of snow on his hair and shoulders.

"Is it snowing?" Kate asked.

"Just started," he said, brushing at the flakes on his jacket. "I don't think it will last long though."

He sat down next to her on the wooden bench.

"So, do you have a lot to do this afternoon when we get back?" she asked. Mentally, she ran through the past seven texts she had gotten from Mrs. Hall while she was gone.

"Quite a few things yet. This time of year at the resort

there is always plenty to do. I will have to check in on several VIP guests and make sure the banquet room is set up for a large party, among a few other odds and ends." He pulled his gloves off one finger at a time and shoved them deep into his coat pocket. "How about you?"

Kate waved her phone lightly. "My list is growing by the minute. Between Mrs. Hall and Jake, I should finish today's assignments sometime after..." She pretended to look at an imaginary watch on her wrist. "...January twelfth."

Luca tipped his head, angling toward her on the bench. "May I ask you something, Ms. Curtis?"

The formal way he addressed her sounded strange, but she realized he hadn't called her by name the whole morning, and they hadn't had an opportunity to discuss anything different.

She must have frowned because he seemed to repent of his question and straightened in his seat.

"I'm sorry. I guess I should mind my own business."

"No, no," Kate said maybe a little too quickly, putting her hand on his forearm for just a second and then pulling it away. She shook her head. "I was just thinking... well, I mean, you called me *Ms. Curtis,* and I was thinking how weird it sounded... you know, since I call you by your first name. I mean, I don't even know your last name, so that makes sense—well, I imagine you probably don't want guests to know your last name for privacy reasons—but I just mean—" She pulled in a deep breath, realizing that she probably sounded like a babbling idiot. Exhaling it all at once, she closed her eyes and began again, slower. "Would you mind calling me Kate, or would that be crossing the line of professionalism?" She opened just one eye and peeked at him, inwardly cringing at her own apparent lunacy.

A brilliant wide smile spread over his face. "I would love to… *Kate.*"

"Phew. Okay." Kate allowed her other eye to open, and she grinned at him. "Thank you."

"So, about the question…" Luca began.

"Oh! Yes, of course!" She leaned forward in interest.

Luca stared at her for a moment, seeming to rethink his petition. Took a breath as if to start, then just as quickly closed his mouth and continued to look at her.

Kate shifted in her seat with a sudden jolt of nervous energy. She giggled. Then sat up straight again, staring right back at him. She tilted her head in confusion.

"Um, what's the question?"

Luca exhaled in evident resolve. "Mr. Adams… um, *Jake.* You can feel free not to answer if it's too personal, but there seems to be some intense disdain for the man whenever he comes up in conversation."

Kate looked down at her jeans and picked a piece of lint off her knee, then brushed twice at the fabric for good measure. "Hmm, *intense disdain.* That's a very astute observation actually. Though I use the term *passionate revulsion* myself." She looked at Luca again. "I'm sorry. I'm not sure what the questions was."

"Oh, yes, I am just wondering if there is a specific reason for it. Again… you don't have to answer if it's too personal. I was just curious and, frankly, a little afraid. I wouldn't want to find myself on the wrong side of your favor."

"Well, if you want the whole story, we have a two-hour train ride ahead of us. But the short version is that I thought he was someone entirely different than he actually is, and luckily, I figured out the truth before anything irreparable happened, and now I simply find him a vile and disgusting human being."

"Good enough," said Luca.

The train clattered to a stop and the squeal of the brakes outside the station doors brought their attention back to the task at hand.

"I'll get the cart, if you will carry my case," Luca said, handing her his brown leather messenger bag.

"Deal." Kate took it from him, and together they boarded the train.

IT WAS CLOSE TO two o'clock when Kate knocked on Mrs. Hall's door. The bellhop waited behind her with the cart of luggage.

When the door swung open, Jake stood in the threshold, resting his forearm on the door frame. "Hello, Kate. Miss me?" He winked and blew her a kiss.

Kate's stomach churned. If she had eaten lunch, there might have been an incident, so she thanked God for the small favor.

"Jake," she said in a flat greeting, then waited for him to move.

He didn't.

"May we come in please? We have your luggage."

The hint of impatience wasn't lost on him, and Jake made a great showing of taking his sweet time to step back and open the door just wide enough for them the pass through with the cart. Then he called over his shoulder in a sing-songy voice, "Oh, Mother, Kate is back."

From somewhere in the suite, Kate heard Mrs. Hall mutter something incomprehensible, and then she appeared striding purposefully into the room, with two hands up to her ear, clasping her earring. "It's about time. I expected you a half an hour ago, Kate."

Kate knew better than to offer an excuse. She led the bellhop into the room and let him unload the cart.

"All your luggage is in order. I double-checked the claim tickets myself." She pointed at the cart.

"And the other things we discussed?"

"All taken care of."

"Good." She pointed to the side door and addressed the bellhop. "Put the silver cases in there. The blue cases can go in the other room." She turned back to Kate. "I told you I was meeting a few people for dinner, didn't I, Kate? That will be in the resort's private banquet room at 6:30. I'll need my azure evening dress cleaned and pressed right away, and I need you to get on the phone with Paige in New York and have her send the sketches from Milan over to Roger. I want them ready to put on my models the day after Christmas."

So much for Mrs. Hall's vacation. Something must have happened today to motivate such a jump on the upcoming line. Kate scribbled the notes into her phone as Mrs. Hall continued, who rattled off three more tasks before abruptly changing the subject.

"Oh, before I forget, there's a Christmas ball here on the 23rd. I will need a gown. I know I didn't pack anything suitable for the occasion."

"There's a dress shop in town—*Dresses by Linda*, I think. I overheard Anne Hathaway and her assistant talking about it in the lobby yesterday. Rumor has it, Linda dresses several of the stars. She may have something that will work," Kate offered.

"Oh, is Anne here? I haven't seen her since last spring." Then more to the point, "I have never heard of *Dresses by Linda*. Are you sure that's the name? What's her last name? Really, Kate, you should have mentioned that to me last night. When it comes to fashion, I should never be the last to know."

"I don't know her last name. I saw the shop yesterday when I was in the village, but I didn't go in, and honestly, I didn't think about it again until I saw Ms. Hathaway and her assistant in the lobby."

"Well, I don't want one of her gowns. If she's as well-known as you say she is, and I am seen in one of her designs instead of my own, I'll be a laughingstock. Not to mention the backlash it might have on my business. No. I hate to do this to you, Kate, but you'll have to find me something I can wear without shame."

"This afternoon?" Kate tried to cover the frustration in her voice, with only a small degree of success. Fortunately, Mrs. Hall either didn't notice or didn't care about Kate's tone.

"No. Not today. Tomorrow is fine. There are too many things I need you to attend to here this afternoon. Go ahead and get started on the list I gave you, and I will meet you back here at six." She waved Kate toward the door, then as an afterthought, added, "See if you can get me a hair appointment for the afternoon of the 23rd. Get whoever is best in town, and I'll need them to come here. Oh, and while you're making calls, I'll need to see Dr. Stucki the moment we get back to New York. Set that up for me, won't you?"

And there it was. The dermatologist appointment Kate had known was coming. Luckily, she had Dr. Stucki's number in her Favorites.

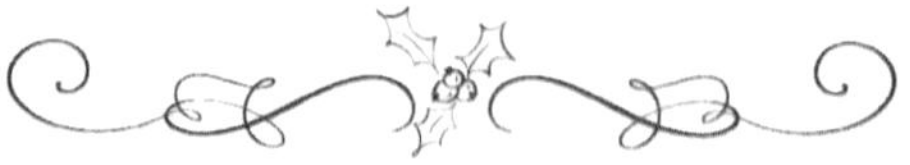

THE AFTERNOON WAS A whirlwind of phone calls and errands. After delivering Mrs. Hall's evening dress to the suite, Kate ran back to her room and dressed for dinner. She slipped into her charcoal halter midi dress, and swept her hair up into a French roll, quickly touched up her lipstick, and grabbed the charcoal scalloped mid-heels from the closet. She draped her evening shawl over her shoulders, tucked her card key and phone into her clutch, and hurried out the door.

Her stomach growled as she closed the door behind her. Dinner could not come soon enough. All she'd had to eat all day was a bagel at the airport and a bag of crackers on the train. Why had she not eaten when Luca suggested lunch before they returned to the resort? Oh, that's right. Because Mrs. Hall had been waiting on her luggage…

She made her way back to Mrs. Hall's suite and knocked on the door two minutes before six.

"You just can't stay away, can you, Kate?" Jake oozed with false charm as he let her into the room. "And I see you've dressed to kill. All this for little old me?"

Kate didn't even try to hide it when she rolled her eyes

this time.

Jake's tie draped loosely around his collar, and he seemed in no rush to finish dressing for dinner as he lifted a bottle of expensive beer to his lips.

"Are you planning to join your mother for dinner this evening?"

"You'd like that, wouldn't you?"

Mrs. Hall strode into the room. "Jake! What have you been doing all this time? We are the hosts! We can't be late for our own dinner party."

"I can't get the knot right." His voice was whiney, like a five-year-old who should know how to tie his shoes but wants his mama to do it for him.

"Kate, will you fix his tie please? I just had my nails done."

Jake's smirk told her that was exactly the result he had wanted.

She shook off the chill of revulsion and did what she was asked, refusing to look him in the eyes, and fighting off the impulse to strangle him with his own tie.

"Little tight, Kate. Trying to shut off my oxygen supply?" Jake tugged at his collar.

Kate returned his earlier smirk to tell him that *that* was exactly what *she* had wanted.

"Everyone ready?" Mrs. Hall asked, returning briskly to the room. "Let's go to dinner."

MRS. HALL'S DINNER PARTY was a successful affair. She had

chosen a menu of seven fashionable courses, culminating in a gourmet *foie gras*. Her guests raved about her gown, and they discussed the upcoming holiday ball with great excitement. Of course, Mrs. Hall promised them her gown would be the stuff of legends.

No pressure, Kate.

When the evening was over, they headed back to the suite. In the lobby, Jake made a quick excuse about meeting someone for drinks, blew a kiss at Kate, and quickly disappeared into the bar.

Mrs. Hall was in the middle of telling Kate the schedule for the following day when out of the corner of Kate's eye, she caught the motion of someone moving toward them.

"Oh my word!" A thin, sleek brunette gasped and stepped closer, stopping right in front of Kate and Mrs. Hall. "Are you—? Are you Cynthia Skye-Adams?" Her eyes were practically bulging out of her head, and she clutched her throat as if she feared she might have a heart attack at any moment.

Mrs. Hall offered that half-pleased, half-mortified smile she made when she was pretending to be humble about who she was. As if anyone who knew anything about fashion for the last thirty years wouldn't recognize her. Kate knew her employer used her husband's last name to give the appearance of wanting her privacy, but secretly Mrs. Hall was more than pleased to have someone recognize her just as this woman was doing now. Kate knew that, later, Mrs. Hall would talk about how embarrassing it was and how she was hoping that just this once she could have remained incognito, but Kate also knew the truth—Mrs. Hall would have been upset and disappointed for days had no one noticed her.

"Yes, that is correct. Do you follow fashion?"

The brunette pushed her way further between the two, interposing herself directly in front of Kate, and cast a nasty glance over her shoulder at her. "Excuse me, you're in my space." Then she turned back to Mrs. Hall with the sweetest smile. "I have always been a huge fan of your work, Ms. Skye-Adams, as you can see." She waved her hand, gesturing from her own head to her toes, showcasing the entire ensemble she was wearing. Every last piece of her outfit was from Mrs. Hall's latest line.

Kate cringed inwardly. While Mrs. Hall did love to be recognized, she did not love fangirls. They drew far too much undignified attention, and she was on vacation with her peers. This conversation was already on its last legs, and Kate was the one who would have to put a stop to it. Mrs. Hall hated to be seen as the bad guy in public. That was Kate's job.

It was in her contract.

"I'm Abigail Steppe..." The woman angled herself closer and thrust out her hand to take Mrs. Hall's. "Do you have new bridal designs? I'm getting married and I've been positively *dying* to get my hands on one of your original wedding gowns!"

Kate sidestepped the woman and inserted herself between the two, cutting off the assault. "I'm sorry, Ms. Steppe, Ms. Skye-Adams has a prior engagement to attend to, but if you give me your business card, we can get in touch later to send you a few samples of her latest work, maybe discuss the possibility of an exclusive design." She turned to Mrs. Hall. "We really must be going; you'll be late for your interview."

Of course, it was a lie. Mrs. Hall had nothing on the night's agenda beyond a glass of red wine and a long bubble bath.

"I'm so sorry, my dear," Mrs. Hall said, shaking her head and offering the signature pout from her modeling days. "The fashion world never sleeps, you know." She smiled and twiddled her fingers in a goodbye, then made a beeline for the elevator.

Abigail Steppe sighed and stared after her for a moment, then she scowled at Kate like she wasn't sure why she was still looking at her. "What are you looking at?"

"Would you like to leave your contact information for Ms. Skye-Adams?"

"With you? I don't think so. I'm Abigail Steppe. I don't deal with underlings." With that she pivoted on her designer Cynthia Skye-Adams pumps, tossed her mousy brown hair over her shoulder, and disappeared into the bar. A faint squeal and the words "Where's my Bride Tribe!?" wafted back to the lobby.

Kate only stared after her in disbelief.

"What just happened?" a voice behind her whispered. It was Luca.

Kate whispered back. "I'm not exactly sure... Apparently, Abigail Steppe doesn't deal with people in my caste."

"Who is Abigail Steppe?"

"I have no blessed idea."

"Whoever she is, she had better hope Bernard didn't witness that little scene."

"Why? What would Bernard do?"

"Bernard is the pillow chocolate guy."

"You have a pillow chocolate guy?"

"Well, he does have other duties."

"Why exactly should Abigail Steppe be afraid of the pillow chocolate guy?" Kate, still whispering.

"He has *special* chocolates for *special* guests." A conspiratorial smirk stretched Luca's lips. "They never know what hit them." He winked and left Kate to figure out what he had meant by that.

When it dawned on her, she frowned, then ran after him. "Luca, hey, what are the chances Bernard will pay a visit to Jake Adams?"

"If I had to guess, he already has."

THE DAY HAD BEEN insanely long and exhausting, but Kate couldn't sleep. Her mind was too busy mulling over the events of the day and second-guessing every conversation she'd had.

And then there was Luca. The memory of his face filled her mind. She barely knew him, and yet he was monopolizing her thoughts. The day had started out under a shadow of suspicion where he was concerned—she cringed at the memory of her sweats and lop-sided bun and the chance meeting in the elevator—but by the end of it, he had become a fixture in her reflection of the day. His presence in her life felt natural somehow. Like she'd always known him.

Kate tossed and turned for an hour under the burden of her thoughts before she finally decided to get up and do something constructive with the time. The bedside clock read 1:17. She grabbed her sketchbook and pencils, wrapped up in a fuzzy robe and snuck out into the hallway. There was a fireplace in the lobby surrounded by comfortable chairs. That was where she headed.

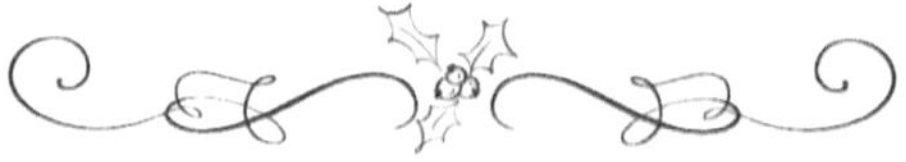

LUCA LOGGED OUT OF his computer and pushed back from the desk. His watch read 1:30. Every muscle in his body screamed for sleep. He had been up and working since five o'clock the morning before. One last walk through the lobby, and he would head downstairs for a few hours of sleep. Then do it all again tomorrow.

He said good night to the night clerk then glanced around the lobby. Not much stirring. There were a few people still in the bar, but everything appeared under control. Out of the corner of his eye, he saw two fuzzy white slippers kicking softly off the edge of one of the overstuffed wingback chairs by the fireplace.

There usually weren't guests hanging out in their pajamas in the lobby, so he decided to investigate. If the guest was drunk and lost, he would help her find her way back to where she belonged.

"Excuse me, *mademoiselle*. Is everything alright here?"

The feet stopped kicking, and a familiar face peered up at him and grinned.

"Ms. Curtis?" he began, then caught his mistake in the reflection of her eyes. "Kate. I would have thought you'd be asleep by now. You've had a busy day."

She shook her head. "Couldn't sleep, so I decided to

do some—" She rolled her hand to the side revealing a sketch of a half-finished clothing design.

"Working this late?"

"It's not technically work. And I couldn't sleep anyway."

Luca took the sketchbook and studied it. He flipped through some of the pages. What he found there was an amazing portfolio of fashion designs. He was no expert, of course, but he could tell she had a knack for it.

"These are really good." He handed the book back to her.

She accepted it from him and flipped back to her spot, avoiding his gaze. "Thank you."

Luca didn't know what to make of her humility. He furrowed his brow. Kate was clearly talented, but she seemed so embarrassed by praise of her work. Maybe his time at this resort had jaded him, but he had never known anyone with as much talent as Kate seemed to have who was as uncomfortable with accolades as she was.

"What does Mrs. Hall say?"

Kate's gaze shot to his face, a look of abject terror flashed there, like he was threatening to grab her sketches and run them right up to Mrs. Hall's room this minute, and just as quickly the look disappeared.

"She won't look at them." Her attention returned to the sketch.

"Won't look at them?"

"Mrs. Hall doesn't accept unsolicited sketches. It's pretty standard procedure."

"But you want to be a designer, don't you? How will you break in if she never sees your work?"

"I thought when I first started working for her, it

would be an easy hurdle. Eventually, she'd have to see my stuff. But it's been five years, and I've kind of lost hope, you know?"

"That's a shame. The world of fashion is missing out." He lay a hand on her shoulder, and when she looked up at him, he thought he saw tears threatening there in her shining green eyes. He withdrew his hand and sat on the arm of the couch.

"What if she has to look?"

Kate raised an eyebrow in question. "What do you mean?"

"Well, I was thinking, maybe something could be arranged where she doesn't have any choice but to see your designs."

Her brow furrowed and she turned to gaze into the fire as if in thought.

"She wants a gown for the ball. She asked me to find her something... Maybe I could pick up a gown, design some alterations... if it passes the Cynthia Skye-Adams test, and she wears it, she's bound to ask who designed it, and then..."

"And then she'll ask to see your portfolio."

Kate's eyes lit up. "That might work!" Then she cringed just a little. "But..."

"Uh-oh. What? What's that look?"

"I'll need an escort to the city. Do you suppose Peter will be available?"

"I don't think you'd have to go all the way into the city. There's a shop here in town."

"*Dresses by Linda?*"

Luca nodded. "That's the one."

Kate shook her head. "She won't even let me go in

there. It's a whole big thing."

"I see." He rubbed his chin in thought. "There's another town just over the mountain. There might be a place there. I can check with Roald. And as far as an escort goes, you shall just have to make do with me once again. I hope you're not too disappointed."

"I guess I can take one for the team," Kate said, and her smile warmed him.

CHAPTER FIVE
Strike the Harp and Join the Chorus

"TODAY IS MY SPA DAY, SO I won't be near the phone at all. Once you've secured my gown for the ball, I'll leave the rest of the day to you." Mrs. Hall lounged on her sofa sipping a cup of tea. "Jake assures me he has a full day of his own planned, so we won't need you. You go ahead and treat yourself to some fun. We are on vacation, after all." She smiled sweetly and paused to leave room for Kate to express undying gratitude.

"Thank you, Mrs. Hall. That's so nice of you," Kate responded as she knew was expected. She did not, however, tell Mrs. Hall about the details of her plan to secure the requested gown. No use in giving the woman information she wouldn't be able to handle. Kate glanced at her watch. Luca would be waiting for her. "Is there anything else?"

"No. You may go. It's almost time for my massage."

Mrs. Hall seemed far too relaxed for someone whose spa day had yet to begin. Kate wondered exactly what was in that tea. Wasn't Wyoming a medical-use only state?

But she had no intention of sticking around to find out.

"SHE WANTS AN EVENING gown for the Christmas ball, but I know she won't wear anything that isn't an original." Kate pulled aside one of the gowns on the rack to get a better look. Everything here, while stylish and beautiful, was mass-produced. Mrs. Hall would know that with a glance.

"Will it work to alter something like this?" Luca suggested, pointing to the mannequin draped with a gorgeous full-length off-the-shoulder sheath gown in gold chiffon.

"That might work. I won't have the time to do it myself though, not with all the stuff Mrs. Hall finds for me to do. Are there any seamstresses or modistes in Huckleberry Falls, I mean, other than in *Dresses by Linda*?"

"I'm sure there is. Let me call Roald and find out." He pulled his phone out of his jacket pocket and stepped outside the shop to make his call.

Kate strode closer to the mannequin in the gold chiffon. It would look amazing on Mrs. Hall. Of course, it would need a few modifications. Kate reached into her purse for her idea notebook and pencil and began to sketch the dress with the changes that had popped into her head.

"Excuse me," a female voice came from the far side of the shop. "Do you have anything in the back that isn't already on display? I'm looking for this—this blue poufy dress, the color of ice. I need it for the royalty crowning ceremony."

Kate glanced toward the voice, pausing in her sketch for just a moment. A woman stood at the counter a few feet away speaking to the salesclerk. The gold chiffon was beautiful, to be sure, and would work for Kate's needs, but if there were other things in the back, perhaps she should take a look first.

"No, I'm sorry, Ms. Klausse. Everything we have is already on display."

The young woman's expression sank, but she nodded at the salesclerk and seemed to force a smile. "Thanks anyway. I'll just find something else."

Kate turned back to the gold chiffon and her sketch, trying to focus on her concept. The woman stopped beside her, studying the gold gown, head tipped thoughtfully to the side.

"It's beautiful," Kate offered, even though it was the very dress she was considering.

"It is. I just—I have this stupid vision in my head, you know? Nothing else is working." The girl turned to her, big brown eyes sparkling. "I sound crazy."

"No, not at all. I totally get it."

The woman grinned. "I'm Cleo. Love love love *your* dress, by the way. It's amazing. Where'd you get it? —if you don't mind my asking."

Kate glanced down at her own attire. She was wearing the ivory mid-thigh sweater dress of her own design with taupe leggings and knee-high boots. It was one of her winter-weather favorites.

"Actually, I designed it," she said. A twinge of embarrassment warmed her cheeks. "I'm Kate, by the way. Nice to meet you." Kate mentally kicked herself. If she was ever going to make it in the fashion world, she was going to have to get over that pesky humility and own her talents. That was precisely why she was still Mrs. Hall's personal assistant instead of working on the design floor.

"You're a designer? That's so cool!" Cleo's bright eyes lit up her face. She glanced over her shoulder for a second, then lifted her hand to the side of her mouth and whispered conspiratorially, "If there's one thing this shop is lacking, it's a designer."

Kate wanted to tell Cleo that all she'd ever wanted to do was be a designer. She wanted to tell her that she had been working for Cynthia Skye-Adams for years, hoping the fashion mogul would notice she had talent. She wanted to show Cleo her portfolio and get her opinion. But she didn't do any of those things. Instead, she smiled and turned back to the gold chiffon sheath gown.

"I am participating in the Christmas royalty pageant in Huckleberry Falls," Cleo said, once again pulling Kate's attention from her sketch. "I waited too long and now I'm having a difficult time finding a dress. I have a picture in my mind of what I want, but nothing in here is quite right."

Kate studied Cleo's face. She recognized the struggle there. Kate had felt it often enough. When you want something so bad, but it seems just out of reach. Her heart went out to the girl. She scanned the racks around them until one caught her eye. Something the color of ice.

"What about that one?" She gestured toward the

glacier blue fabric peeking out between a scarlet mermaid gown and a vermillion A-line. "Is that the color you were thinking of?"

Cleo's gaze followed Kate's finger to the rack on their left. The moment she found what Kate was showing her, her whole face lit up with excitement.

"Yes! Yes! That is the exact color!" In three long strides she was at the rack, pulling the two red dresses to each side so she could maneuver the blue gown to the front.

It was a gorgeous shade of blue. It had a long waist and a bouffant skirt. Kate knew with just one look that Cleo would look amazing in that dress.

"It is the perfect color. And I do like the way the bodice and skirt are." Cleo's eyebrows drew together in a pensive scowl. "It's probably the closest I'm going to get to the image I have in my head."

"What if—" Kate began, then thought better of it, though ideas for the gown flew through her mind at a dizzying pace. Designing alterations for Cleo would take time, and as much as she loved the prospect of the project, she knew Mrs. Hall's 24-7 demands would make it impossible. Plus, she didn't even know if there was a local modiste who would be willing to take on the job.

As if on cue, the bell on the shop door chimed, and Luca returned, frowning.

"So, Roald said there was another seamstress in Huckleberry Falls, but she retired two years ago." He nodded a silent greeting at Cleo, then fixed his gaze on Kate. "I know it's not ideal, but if it helps, I can track down any tools or machines, or whatever you need to do the alterations."

Deflated, Kate shook her head. There wouldn't be

time. Not if Mrs. Hall and Jake kept her as busy as they had over the last couple of days. The whole airline-losing-the-luggage fiasco, while amusing at first, had made Kate's schedule even more unbearable. "I appreciate it, but there is no way Mrs. Hall will give me that kind of uninterrupted time." She knew this one afternoon would not be enough time, and even with Mrs. Hall telling her she was free to do what she wanted, there was a distinct possibility that that *tea* would wear off in a couple of hours, and Mrs. Hall would change her mind.

"Even if she knew what it was for?"

"Are you kidding me? Mrs. Hall would never allow me to design something for her. I'm untried as far as she's concerned. An unacceptable risk. No. She can't know. She probably thinks I'm asking Paige to overnight her one of her new gowns."

"That's ridiculous."

"Tell me about it." Kate turned back to the gold gown and slid the fabric between her thumb and forefinger sadly. Her vision for the gown would never happen now.

"Wait..." It was Cleo. "Are you talking about Mrs. Stradley?" She was talking to Luca.

"That's right. Do you know her?" Luca raised his eyebrows.

"Yeah! She does a lot of volunteering at the animal sanctuary. I see her all the time."

A spark of hope flared in Kate's heart. "Do you think she would be willing to work with me? I mean... does she have the time?"

"I'm almost certain she'd do it. In fact, I'll call her right now." The light in the girl's smile fanned the spark into a flame of hope.

Kate watched as Cleo slid her phone out of her purse and tapped on the screen. As she put the phone to her ear and took a couple steps away, Kate turned to Luca and grabbed his forearm, unable to contain her own excitement. "Can you believe this? What an amazing girl!"

"That's exactly what I was thinking," Luca said, but his eyes were locked on Kate's, and she couldn't help but think they weren't talking about the same person.

Perhaps it was just wishful thinking.

Hope had a way of multiplying itself, even when it wasn't warranted.

Kate let her hand drop from his arm abruptly.

When Cleo turned back to them, the brightness of her expression was encouraging. "Okay, so I talked to Mrs. Stradley, and she would be happy to meet with you to discuss what you want to do. She said she has too much time on her hands and would love a project."

"That's fantastic!" Kate said.

"Here. I'll give you her number." She glanced back to her phone. Her eyes widened in alarm at something she saw there. "Oh crap! I have to go!" She scribbled down the phone number on a piece of paper and thrust it toward Kate. "I'm so sorry to rush out like this. Mrs. Stradley is expecting to hear from you. Just tell her Cleo gave you her number." She hung the ice blue gown back on the rack and tucked it in deep between two others. "I'll have to come back for this." Cleo waved at Kate and headed for the door. "It was nice to meet you!" And she was gone.

Kate glanced up at Luca. He shrugged as if he wasn't sure what just happened. Then he pointed at the slip of paper she held.

"Would you like me to call for you?"

"No, I can do it. Thank you."

She dialed the number and waited for Mrs. Stradley to answer. Her eyes traced the rack of gowns until it stopped on the ice blue dress Cleo had left behind.

"Hello, this is Kate Curtis. Cleo gave me your number. I was wondering if you had time to do some alterations for me… yes, that's right… Actually, there will be *two* gowns."

AFTER KATE AND LUCA left Mrs. Stradley's house, Kate was almost giddy. Mrs. Stradley had agreed to do a rush job on both dresses. The two ladies had gone over her designs, and Mrs. Stradley's enthusiasm for the project was more than Kate could have asked for. Her creative energy spilled over into her mood, and she found herself almost bouncing down the sidewalk with excitement.

"Are you ready to go back to the resort?" Luca asked, eyeing her.

"I'm too excited to go back yet. Would you mind just dropping me off in town?" she asked. "Mrs. Hall has given me the afternoon to myself, and I don't know how much time I have before she comes to her senses and calls me back in."

He cast a glance toward the direction of the village center and frowned. Was he disappointed? When his gaze returned to hers, there was a spark of mischief in his eyes.

"Well, I could do that, of course. But I might have a better idea."

"Don't you have to get back?"

"I won't tell if you won't."

Kate giggled. "What did you have in mind?" She bounced lightly on her feet, hardly able to contain herself. The way her day had come together, bringing her a huge step closer to her dream of becoming a designer, made her heart happy, and that was translating as electric energy to the rest of her body.

Above her was a wire strut holding up an awning, laden with snow. An awning positioned directly over where Kate and Luca stood, as luck would have it.

Bouncing in high heel boots, though stylish, was ill-advised. Kate lost her balance. She was forced to catch herself… grabbing hold of the only thing that was within reach. The ill-fated wire strut.

The awning collapsed, dumping several pounds of ice-cold snow unceremoniously onto Luca's head.

Maybe it was the nervous energy—maybe it was the priceless look of shock and mortification on Luca's face—but Kate couldn't help herself. She shrieked with laughter.

"You think that's funny, do you?" Luca said, raising a frosty eyebrow, as he grabbed a handful from the pile of damp snow on his shoulder. Slowly, he lowered the clump of snow and began to methodically form it into a small white ball.

Just right for throwing.

"Now, wait…" Kate said, suddenly breaking off from her laughter. A thrill of fear shot through her. "What are you going to do with that?"

"Oh, nothing much," he said, narrowing his eyes. Luca cocked his arm back into position.

"No, no, no! Don't you dare!" she squealed and jumped off the sidewalk into the yard, trying to dodge the inevitable.

When the snowball hit the tree just ahead of her, it disintegrated on impact, spraying snow in a wide circular pattern. She tossed a glance over her shoulder, barely able to keep upright, but hoping Luca would have no chance with a moving target. He scooped up another handful and chased after her, laughing.

"Come back here!"

Kate stumbled but somehow managed to keep her feet under her. These boots were not made for running. Heck, they weren't even made for snow; she could already feel the melting ice seeping in through the leather and spreading through the fibers of her socks.

Another snowball whizzed by her ear, catching a wayward strand of hair and lacing it with snowflakes. She shrieked, turning to look behind her again, just in time to take a direct hit to the face. Snow everywhere. Her foot came to an abrupt stop, hooking on a root or something hard buried under the snow, but her body kept moving forward. She twisted in the air and managed to land squarely on her rear in the middle of a well-placed snow berm. Dazed, she sputtered and spit clumps of snow out of her mouth.

Luca caught up to her, laughing, and working to catch his breath. He bent at the waist and rested his hands on his knees. "There. Now we're even," he said as he offered a hand to help her up.

Through the snowflakes coating her eyelids, Kate saw a blurry grin, the only evidence of his mischievous intent.

"Even?" she breathed. "Hardly. Mine was an accident." She glanced at the pile of snow at her side, making a sudden decision. Before Luca could react, Kate scooped a giant handful and forced it into his face, taking care to rub it in a circular motion, effectively whitewashing his perfectly beautiful Swiss features. Then she spun around onto her hands and knees and lunged away to escape his grasp.

She almost made it.

He leapt toward her, grabbing her heel, but their combined momentum brought them both sliding forward and firmly into the base of a nearby tree—a tree, as luck would have it, whose branches were fully despondent with the unbearable weight of wet, ice-cold December snow.

Kate rolled over to see the branches bending almost vertical and the snow sliding toward her at a fantastic speed. Luca traced her horrified gaze upward, his eyes widened just in time to take the brunt of the avalanche full in the face.

Down it came, half-burying the pair in ice and snow.

Kate squealed as the ice made its way down the neck of her sweater, trickling down her spine. She shook her head and brushed at the snow coating her face and chest. It was freezing.

"See? Now… *now* we're even," she said with a shiver.

The rumble of Luca's laughter caught her off-guard. She opened her eyes to find Luca's face just inches from her own. His eyes were closed tight, and there were particles of snow and ice covering his face, clinging to his hair, eyebrows, and eyelashes. His laughter subsided and he opened his eyes, meeting her gaze.

Neither of them moved for a moment.

Luca's gaze bore into hers. Kate couldn't do anything but stare back, trying desperately to keep from getting lost in the deep dark blue of his eyes. So when his gaze darted to her mouth and then back to her eyes, she knew what he was thinking, and she found her own gaze wandering to his lips and her mind entertaining the thought of kissing him, and an urgent desire for it rose in her chest.

The voice of reason nagged in the back of her mind.

This can't happen. You can't fall for this guy. You're leaving. You'll be gone in a few days. This can't happen.

Kate knew it was true. Even the wise thing to do. Stop this before it started. But she didn't want to, and it felt like she was being tempted beyond what she was able to handle. Where was her escape?

She didn't want an escape.

Or maybe Luca *was* the escape from the drudgery her life had become.

Would it be so bad?

Luca's eyes traced the path to her lips again.

Kate was rapidly falling under his spell.

But then...

Her phone chirped impatiently, effectively breaking the trance and jolting Kate back into real life. She sat up suddenly, narrowly missing Luca, who dodged the blow with the reflexes of a cat.

"It's Mrs. Hall." Kate's heart sank. "She says it's an emergency." She turned her head to face Luca. "How far to the emergency room?"

His eyes widened in alarm, and he jumped to his feet and offered her his hand to help her up. "I can take you. It's just a couple miles from here."

CHAPTER SIX
Troll the Ancient Yuletide Carol

SIX AND A HALF HOURS.

That's how long Kate had sat in the ER waiting for Jake's head to be stitched up.

Apparently, in Wyoming, the rich and beautiful people still had to wait their turn. Of course, Jake had thought that the epitome of injustice, and made sure everyone within earshot knew it.

Mrs. Hall had opted to stay at the resort.

It *was* an emergency.

But it was an emergency Kate could easily handle on her own.

That was what Mrs. Hall said.

That and, "Make sure he gets the best care, Kate. Stay with him the whole time. This is an emergency that requires your *personal* touch. I would just be in the way there. You know how I get when I'm in a hospital."

Of course, she wasn't wrong.

Mrs. Hall would have been a bigger baby about it than Jake had been.

"Don't let them scar me, Kate, will you? Make sure they call in the plastic surgeon. I don't want these butchers making a mess of my face."

One would think he had needed major reconstructive surgery the way he talked.

He had a tiny cut on his forehead, just deep and long enough to need four stitches. And how did he get it? From paying too much attention to the backside of a woman walking past him and not nearly enough attention to the guy carrying skis on his shoulder crossing the path in front of him.

When they finally returned to the resort, it was late. She dropped Jake off at his suite and went to her room.

Even though she had missed dinner and was hungry, Kate just wanted to get out of her wet socks and boots, maybe sit in the quiet for a few minutes before facing the world again.

She sat heavily on the bed and pulled off her boots. They were probably ruined. Kate's mind replayed the afternoon in the snow as she peeled her still very wet socks off one by one and tossed them onto the floor beside her boots.

Lying back onto the pillow, Kate allowed her body to relax. In spite of the way it had ended, it had been one of the best days Kate had experienced in a long time. She allowed her eyes to close, the memory of Luca's face so close to hers danced in her mind, and the warmth that accompanied the thought comforted her until sleep pulled her under.

THE CLOCK ON THE table beside her said 12:37 A.M. when Kate's eyes popped open. The only sound in the room was the rumble of her stomach, roaring its protest against skipping dinner.

She sat up groggily and rubbed her eyes, trying to get her bearings.

The restaurant was closed.

Room service, of course, was not an option down in the bowels of the resort.

Kate sighed. Why hadn't she bought some groceries? There was a whole little kitchenette in her room.

When would you have had time for grocery shopping?

"It doesn't do me any good to wonder about that now," Kate thought aloud. She glanced again at the clock and swung her legs over the bed. She was still wearing her sweater dress and leggings. Her socks and boots lay on the floor where she had left them.

First order of business, change clothes. Second, drink some water. Maybe that would take the edge off the hunger.

It didn't.

She wouldn't be able to go back to sleep now.

Not hungry.

The clock read 12:53.

Maybe the lobby bar?

No. They were probably still serving drinks, but the

kitchen had already closed. She drummed her fingertips on the nightstand. Her gaze fell on her phone.

When the thought came to her, she tried to push it out of her mind.

Luca had said to call if she needed anything.

But it was late now. Really late.

He'd had a full day. He was probably sleeping.

Kate's stomach sent a sharp pang of hunger reverberating through her.

On impulse, she grabbed her phone, scrolled through to Luca's number, and pressed *call.*

Luca answered the phone on the second ring. "This is Luca. How may I help you?"

The sound of his accent took her by surprise, causing her to hesitate just a moment before responding. "Um, hey, Luca. This is Kate. Kate Curtis. In Room 17…" She rolled her eyes at her own stupidity. Like he didn't know who she was. He had her number stored in his phone. "Um, you told me to call if I needed anything." It was silent for a moment. "Is this a bad time?" It was too late at night. Maybe he was sleeping. Kate immediately regretted calling him.

"Oh, hey. Kate. How are you? How did it go at the hospital?"

"It went about how you'd expect."

"Is Mr. Adams alright?"

"Honestly, I think his pride is wounded beyond repair, but according to the plastic surgeon, his head should heal just fine."

There was a soft chuckle on the other end of the line.

"Am I calling too late?"

"Not at all. I was just going over the schedule for

tomorrow. With Peter out, I had to shift a couple of things around." There was a pause, then, "I'm sorry, did you say you needed something?"

"Um, yeah, sorry. I'm wondering if I can get something to eat. I kind of missed dinner."

There was another pause on the line.

"I think I can make that happen. One moment, please."

There was a knock on Kate's door. Odd. She hadn't been expecting anyone. She stayed where she was, holding the phone to her ear, waiting for Luca to come back on the line.

"Aren't you going to answer the door?"

"Oh. I... Yes, I suppose I should see who it is. Hang on." Kate moved to the door and peeked through the peephole. On the other side of the door stood a man wearing sweats and a gray T-shirt, with his back to the door. When he turned back toward the door, she realized it was Luca, holding his phone up to his ear.

"It's cold and dark out here," he whispered into the phone.

She opened the door. "I'm sorry. I didn't know it was you."

He laughed. The same soothing sound she had been replaying in her mind all evening.

"We can go up to the kitchen. It's closed for the night, but..." he pulled a card out of his pocket, "I have the key." He punctuated his statement with a wide smile.

Luca led her up the stairs and through a dimly lit hallway until they came to a side exit. Just to the left of the exit, there was a set of double doors. Luca slid his key card into slot and the lock clicked out of place. Luca opened the door and gestured for Kate to precede him into that dark room.

She hesitated. "Are you sure this is okay?"

"No. But I don't think anyone will see us."

Not reassuring in the least.

"Maybe you should go first."

Luca shrugged and stepped in front of her, reached around to the wall and flicked on the switch. It flickered on, and light filled the room.

"Hmm…" Luca said. "Maybe a bit much. We don't want to draw attention." He flicked the light back off and used the flashlight on his phone instead. "Follow me," he said, and stepped inside the kitchen.

Kate reluctantly followed.

The beam from Luca's phone lit the way as they wound around the food prep islands and came to one of the stoves. Luca reached for the switch on the wall and snapped it on. It lit up just one spotlight over the stove top.

"That's better. Now…" He turned off his cell phone light and slipped it into his pocket. Then he rolled up his sleeves. "What are you in the mood for?"

"I… I don't know. I'm just hungry." As if to prove her point, her stomach audibly growled its agreement.

"I make a mean omelet."

"Sure." She could feel the embarrassment heating her cheeks. Luckily, it was dim enough that Luca probably wouldn't notice.

"Omelet it is then." He spun around and opened the walk-in cooler, then disappeared inside for a moment. He returned just as quickly with a bowl of eggs. He set them on the counter next to the stove and then reached over Kate's head for a skillet that hung from the ceiling rack.

"I really appreciate this."

He cracked the eggs into the bowl. "Not at all. It's my job to take care of the resort's guests. You're a guest, aren't you?"

There it was. The subtle reminder that she was a visitor and would be leaving in just a few days. It was his job to be nice.

But it didn't quite add up.

"So, are you saying you bring all the hungry guests down here in the middle of the night?"

"Not exactly. I mean, they wouldn't all fit in the kitchen. And I'm not trained to cook for that many people. Plus, my omelets really aren't that good."

"So, when you said you make a mean omelet, you meant—"

"Unfriendly."

"Wow. You really know how to sell your cooking. Should I be worried? You don't have Bernard hiding in here somewhere with his special chocolates, do you?" Kate glanced around the dark room for suspicious shadows.

He chuckled. "No. You don't put chocolate in omelets, silly." He gently tapped her nose with his index finger, then returned to his cooking.

When it was ready, Luca pulled up a stool for her and slid a steaming dish toward her. Kate sat down and picked up the fork, hesitating briefly.

"It probably won't kill you," Luca said, wearing a playful half-smile.

"Well, that's a relief." Kate inhaled the aroma of the freshly-plated omelet. Her stomach rumbled again. "Do you have any salsa?"

"Salsa? In a Swiss resort?" He snorted in disgust.

"Well, what would you put on it?"

"Swiss omelets are not the same as what you Americans eat. They are very rich. Thicker than French crepes, bigger than pancakes. They can be filled with vegetables and cream sauce or with jam or chocolate syrup." He quirked an eyebrow. "Chocolate syrup. Not pillow chocolates—incidentally, these are filled with spinach and cream." He gestured toward the plate. "Just like mama used to make."

"So… no salsa."

"No. Just try it, Kate."

The sound of her name on his lips thrilled her. She studied his face a moment, wishing he'd say it again.

"Go on." He pointed at her plate.

She looked at the omelet. It did smell amazing. She pinched off a piece with the edge of her fork, scooped it up, and popped it into her mouth.

Luca hadn't exaggerated about its richness. The fullness of flavor brought her full attention to what she was eating. She had never had an omelet like this before, and she knew they were something she could get used to.

"Holy pancakes!"

"Not pancakes, Kate. *Omelet*," Luca said with wide grin.

Kate's gaze shot to his face. "I thought you said these were unfriendly! They are the opposite of that. What is the opposite of that?"

"Friendly?"

"A-ma-zing!" She brought another bite to her mouth. She was certain she could never enjoy a regular American omelet again.

"I'm glad you like it."

She did. She definitely did.

Once every last bite was consumed, she stood and brought her dish around to where Luca stood. "Where should I set this?"

"I'll take it. What do you say about dessert?" He reached for the plate, then stretched beyond her to set it on the counter closer to the sink.

"I don't want to be a bother."

"You're no bother."

When she looked up into his eyes, they were standing much closer than she had anticipated. The heat radiated from—was it the stove or Luca? Kate's brain seemed to swim, finding the memory from earlier in the afternoon, the closeness of Luca in the snow, how much she'd wanted him to kiss her.

Before she knew what she was doing, she stepped closer, willing it to happen before her judgment could make a comeback.

Luca didn't back away, but his eyes held a question. She must have answered it with her own because he lifted his hands to cup her face, holding her gently, and everything seemed to move in slow motion.

His head descended slowly, giving her time to object.

She didn't want to object.

Her lips parted expectantly as he closed the distance almost hesitating before the first soft brush of his soft lips. His first kiss was like an introduction, a question. She almost smiled at how right it felt when his hands moved to her hips gently pulling her against him as their mouths met again, this time more urgent.

Was this really happening?

His kiss was slow and purposeful, burning from the gentle press of his mouth on hers. A shiver rushed down her spine as her mouth trembled beneath his. He deepened the kiss as her hands, with a mind of their own, snaked up around his neck. His fingers raked through her hair as they stumbled backwards against the metal table. A pan crashed to the ground. They jumped apart from one another.

Luca's eyes danced and his chest heaved. Kate quickly averted her eyes and whispered, "So... um..." Her voice was raspy, her breath gone. She cleared her throat. "Can I get the recipe for that omelet?"

CHAPTER SEVEN
Follow Me in Merry Measure

Back in his room, Luca tossed and turned.

He had a problem.

And he knew it was his own fault.

For some reason, he had a thing about falling for women he could never have. First there had been Amelie, his brother's fiancée, now Kate, and she would be leaving in a few days. Gone from his life forever. He shook his head, thinking the motion would erase the memory of her in his arms—at the same time, hoping it wouldn't.

He would see her again. There were too many activities going on this week that would put them together.

What if she wanted to talk about the kiss?

What would he say?

Worse yet, what if she thought it was just his M.O.?

The way he operated. A new woman every week. *It's my job to take care of the resort's guests. You're a guest, aren't you?* He cringed inwardly. Why had he said that?

If she did think that of him, she'd be wrong.

Luca didn't give away his heart easily. He had been guarding it closely since putting the pieces back together, and he didn't relish the idea of repeating the process.

Kate was leaving. It wouldn't pay to get too attached. It would be best to keep his distance. No matter how much he despised the thought.

CAN I GET THE recipe for that omelet?

The memory haunted Kate, charging into her mind the second her alarm went off in the morning, quickly followed by the chirping of her phone with a text from Mrs. Hall.

For once, Kate was happy to have the demand for her attention. "I hope you have a crap ton of work for me today, Mrs. Hall," she thought aloud, pulling up the message on the screen. Words she'd never spoken in her life.

CSA: DRESS FOR BREAKFAST. SEE YOU IN THIRTY MINUTES. LOTS OF ACTIVITIES TODAY!

Thank God. Anything to keep her mind off Luca.

She typed in her acknowledgement and rolled out of bed.

Thirty minutes later, Kate was dressed to impress and knocking on the door of Mrs. Hall's suite.

Mrs. Hall answered the door. "Oh, it's you, Kate. I was

expecting room service. They should be here any minute." She turned and walked back toward her room. "Check into that for me, will you, Kate?"

Kate glanced down the hallway in both directions. No sign of anyone. Stepping into the suite, she let the door close behind her and went to the phone on the desk. She dialed zero and waited.

"This is Luca. How may I help you?"

Kate froze. Tongue-tied. All rational thought vacated her mind, and she stood in silence, desperately racking her brain for words to string together into a coherent sentence.

"Madame Hall? Is everything okay?" His voice held tempered concern.

"Uh, no. I mean, yes… Mrs. Hall is… the cart with the food…" There were words somewhere. She just couldn't find them. She pulled in a deep breath, trying to gather her wits. "Room service." She exhaled the breath all at once. "Um… this is Kate," she finally said, wincing from the pain that was her current state of mind.

There was a palpable silence on the other end of the line. Was he struggling the way she was?

When there was no response, she found her words. "Mrs. Hall asked me to check on her breakfast. Is it on its way?"

Another pause, a throat clearing on the other side, then, "Uh, yes. I can check on that for you, Ms. Curtis. One moment, please."

Ms. Curtis.

Not Kate.

Ms. Curtis.

They had gone back to being formal. As if nothing had happened between them. As if she had crossed a line so sacred that he had no other option but to put her back at arm's length and treat her like the guest she was.

She was so stupid.

Luca returned to the line. "Your room service will arrive momentarily. They just stepped onto the elevator."

"Thank you," Kate said tightly and hung up. Maybe a little more forcefully than she should have.

"Is there a problem?" Mrs. Hall asked, returning to the sitting room, clasping her necklace behind her neck.

"Breakfast is on the way." Kate knew full well that was all that mattered to Mrs. Hall, so there was no use muddying the water with any unnecessary information.

"You seem upset, Kate. Are you sure there's no problem?" She had yet to look at Kate but was instead focused on the clasp of her diamond bracelet. When the struggle proved too frustrating, she held her wrist out toward her assistant. "Kate?"

Kate hooked the bracelet. "Everything is fine." She smiled, hoping it would appear sincere.

"Well, I need you to be entirely focused, Kate, so whatever it is, put it aside until you're on your own time, will you?" Mrs. Hall moved with purpose to the desk and pulled a brochure out of the drawer. "These are the events for today taking place in the village." She turned on her heel and handed it to Kate. "Ordinarily, I don't go in for the festivals of the peasantry, but I feel like we can make an exception here. Don't you?"

Kate opened the brochure and scanned it.

"Word around the resort is that most guests will be attending the festivities, so at the very least, I'll have to make an appearance. Some of it sounds almost fun. There is ice skating in the square and a winter carnival of sorts. A parade at noon. I haven't been to a parade since I was a little girl." Mrs. Hall laughed at her own joke, then took a seat on the couch. "Of course, I'll need an escort. Jake is so strung out on pain medication that he will be of no use today."

A dreadful thought occurred to Kate, and she hoped Mrs. Hall wasn't going to ask her to stay here and keep an eye on Jake. Quick on the heels of that thought came another. Who could she get to escort Mrs. Hall to the village?

There was a knock at the door, and Kate opened it to let room service wheel the cart inside.

"I'm going to have you come with me today. Since you've been to the village a couple of times, you know your way around."

"Will we be taking the shuttle?" Kate asked.

"Oh, no. I didn't think of that. How did you get to village yesterday?"

"One of the managers drove me. Luca."

"Luca?" She appeared deep in thought. "Oh, yes, wasn't he the handsome one with the French accent who checked us in? Mmm, I remember *him*."

The way the last sentence rolled out of Mrs. Hall's mouth made Kate's skin crawl.

"Call down and get him to drive us."

A jolt shot through Kate, setting every nerve on edge, and tying her stomach in knots. She could not ask Luca to drive them. It would look exactly like she was angling to seduce him. Like she thought she had some claim to him, when clearly, she did not.

"It's likely he'll be busy. He's in charge of preparing for the community ball and the resort's Christmas Eve dinner. He only took me because they were shorthanded yesterday. Maybe I can order a car?"

Mrs. Hall looked up at her from her place on the couch. "Busy? Nonsense. I'm an important guest. They'll bend over backward for me." She stared at Kate a moment, then must have thought Kate didn't believe her, abruptly stood and went to the desk phone. She picked it up and dialed.

Kate could only watch in horror.

"Good morning, Renate. I'd like to speak with the manager. What's his name? ...Luca, that's right..." There was a lengthy pause. "Good morning, Luca... yes, I hope you will... I'd like to go into the village today for the festivities... no, I would rather not take the shuttle. Do you have a driver who can escort me? ...oh, I'm sorry to hear that... I was so looking forward to the Christmas celebrations in town. I've heard wonderful things about them; in fact, that's why we chose the Edelweiss Resort for our vacation in the first place. It's sad, we get so few vacations... would you, dear? Oh, that would be wonderful... Thank you. I'll expect to leave in time for the parade." The clatter of the phone on the cradle punctuated her sentence, and she glanced at Kate with a triumphant smirk. "That, my sweet Kate, is how it's done." And she swaggered back to her seat on the couch. "Now, shall we have breakfast?"

THE FIFTEEN-MINUTE DRIVE into the village seemed interminable.

Kate rode in the back seat with Mrs. Hall, but she didn't speak unless she had to. Mrs. Hall was prattling on her speakerphone with Paige about the Milan sketches and the model lineup for the spring show. Kate tried to keep her eyes focused on the notes she was taking from Mrs. Hall's conversation, but every once in a while, her gaze would wander to Luca's reflection in the rearview mirror, where she would catch him looking back at her and quickly avert her eyes.

The phone call ended right before Luca pulled into a parking space.

"Luca," Mrs. Hall said, "have you been to many of these festivals?"

"Yes, madame, I come every year. They're quite enjoyable. The locals put a lot of work into their holiday festivals."

Mrs. Hall tossed a look at Kate. "See, Kate? We weren't pulling him away from business. He was planning to come anyway."

That was not *what he said*, Kate thought, but she didn't bother to argue. She shot a look into the mirror that she hoped seemed apologetic, but Luca wasn't looking.

"That is true, madame, and while I might have come just a little later, I am very happy to have such lovely company."

"Oh…" Mrs. Hall pretended to blush. "Isn't he a charmer, Kate?"

You don't know the half of it. She fought the urge to roll her eyes.

Luca stepped out of the car and opened the back door for Mrs. Hall, offering his hand to help her out. Naturally, she took it, wearing her model smile. He glanced at Kate through the door, as if he wanted to say something but didn't.

Kate got out on her own side and joined Mrs. Hall on the walkway.

"Where is the best place to watch the parade?" Mrs. Hall asked, glancing up and down the street.

The village square was just behind them. Kate could see the carnival booths and people moving in and out of the stalls. There were decorative lanterns laced around the square and, in the distance, a small Ferris wheel.

She swung back around to find Luca watching her.

"Of course, I haven't been here before, but according to the brochure, the parade will come right up the main street and make a loop around the town square, then head back up the back side, ending by the bridge." Kate traced the path through the air with her finger.

Mrs. Hall nodded, then turned to Luca. "What do you think, Luca? Shall we find the perfect place?"

"It would be my pleasure, madame." He offered her his arm, and she hooked her hand in the crook of his elbow, giggling like a schoolgirl at his disgusting Swiss allure.

Kate could feel the fury burning through her as she watched them walk up the street arm-in-arm. And she wasn't sure who she was more upset with—Luca and his proper Swiss *savoir faire*, oozing charm from every pore, or Mrs. Hall and her co-ed style flirting, pretending to be thirty years younger. She glared after them.

The answer was *neither*.

Kate was most upset with herself. How could she have been so stupid?

Mrs. Hall called over her shoulder. "Aren't you coming, Kate?"

Grudgingly, Kate forced herself to follow, and with each step her blood boiled.

They wandered until they found a place Mrs. Hall was convinced was the best spot in the village to watch the parade. A place where she could easily be seen by people gathering in any direction, and her appearance would be noted by anyone who cared about such things.

The parade passed by, as parades often do. Kate hardly noticed any part of it. Luca and Mrs. Hall, on the other hand, hardly seemed to notice Kate, as they laughed and pointed out *all* the things.

By the time the parade was over, Kate had had quite enough for one day.

"Mrs. Hall, if you don't need me, I could go back to the resort and check on Jake," she said as they walked back toward the carnival area. After all, Mrs. Hall had an escort. What could she possibly need with Kate?

But Mrs. Hall ignored her question. Instead she focused intently on the milling throng ahead of them. "Isn't that Anderson Cooper?" She squinted—as if Mrs. Hall would ever be caught doing such a thing. "I think it is! Oh, I must go say hello. Kate, be a dear, and keep our Luca company for a bit, won't you?" She scurried away without another word and disappeared into the carnival crowd.

Our Luca? Kate snorted in disgust.

"Kate..." It was Luca. He stood with his hands in his pockets, studying her.

"Oh, it's *Kate* now, is it?" It was impossible to keep the bite of sarcasm out of her voice.

His eyes widened. "Well, I..."

"I believe it was *Ms. Curtis* this morning, wasn't it? Let's just leave it at that, shall we, Mister... Mister...

Agghh!" She roared in frustration and stamped her foot, balling up her fists at her sides. "Just tell me what your last name is!"

"Burk. Luca Burk," he offered, wide-eyed.

"Thank you!" Kate yelled, maybe a little too forcefully. Then, "Mr. *Burk*!" She worked to channel all her anger into one searing death glare, but the humor behind his eyes and the way his body trembled ever so slightly, as if he was stifling a laugh, made it clear that her *death glare* was not having the desired effect.

Exasperation tore through her, finally erupting in another roar. "Ergghh!" She spun on her heel and charged into the crowd.

"Kate, wait!"

She could hear him calling after her, but she was too angry to face him. No… *humiliated*. That was the word. Tears blurred her vision, slowing her progress through the sea of merry-makers. Blindly, she wound her way through the people and the booths, moving as quickly as she could with no other thought than to escape.

Just a few more steps and she would be through the square, safely on the other side, beyond the Christmas lights, when she felt Luca's grip on her elbow, pulling her to a stop.

"Kate, stop!" he said firmly.

She couldn't look at him. Not now.

THE SITUATION HAD GOTTEN way out of hand. Keeping his

distance hadn't worked. And now the fact that Luca had even tried that strategy was working against him. While he could explain away everything that had happened this morning by saying he was just doing his job, he knew the tears on Kate's face were all his fault.

"I'm sorry, Kate. For everything. I thought... I thought I could make it better by keeping my distance. That if I backed off, I couldn't get too attached. You can see how well that worked out."

Kate wouldn't look at him.

He kept talking anyway, hoping to get through, to say the right thing. "Last night..." he began but hesitated when her gaze shot to his face. The confusion and pain were evident in her eyes. He started again, "Last night took me by surprise. A wonderful, beautiful surprise. But frankly, it was confusing. Clearly, I like you. I enjoy spending time with you. But you'll be leaving in just a few days, and I'm afraid I may already be too invested." There. He'd said it out loud.

Her eyes searched his face, softening just a little.

"I didn't handle the situation well," he said. "I'm sorry."

She stared at him for a moment as if trying to decide if she should speak. "I'm sorry too," she said at last, and her gaze dropped to the ground. "At first, I just felt stupid. Then I actually *was* stupid. I am more upset about that than anything else."

"You weren't stupid." He gently took her hand. It seemed so small in his.

She lifted her head to look at him again. "So... what do we do?"

Luca shook his head. He didn't know how to answer

that. He knew what he *wanted* to do, but he also knew it wasn't going to happen. The real question was what *should* they do. "What do *you* want to do?"

Kate looked over her shoulder toward the carnival, then glanced beyond Luca in the direction of the ice rink. "I want to skate," she finally said, smiling sweetly.

How could he refuse?

CHAPTER EIGHT
While I tell of Christmas Treasure

AFTER SKATING, LUCA AND KATE WANDERED around amidst the carnival booths, played a few games, and tested all the pastries. A few times they spotted Mrs. Hall in the crowd, but she never did come looking for them. She seemed to be in her element, and Kate was glad for the reprieve.

Kate found an empty table while Luca went to get the hot chocolate.

"Did you see the swans?" Luca asked when he returned with two giant steaming mugs of cocoa.

"Swans? In town? You're kidding!"

"One of the food booths has a pen of swans over there." He gestured with his cocoa as he sat down beside her.

"Really? I thought swans were dangerous." She took the offered cup and lifted it to her lips, taking a tiny sip to test the temperature. It burned her tongue.

"I wouldn't be surprised. They seemed pretty mad. Lots of hissing and flapping," Luca said.

"I'm glad they're in a pen. I would not want to meet a flock of swans in a dark alley."

"Not to worry," Luca said with a coy smirk. "There are no dark alleys in Huckleberry Falls."

"But there are swans." Kate could hear them now. They did sound angry, and the noise seemed to be getting closer. When people started screaming and jumping though, she knew there was a real problem. "Um… I don't think those swans are in their pen anymore." She rose to her feet and tried to see what was happening, but there were too many people.

"I think you're right," Luca said.

There was a lot of shouting, and then Kate could hear someone asking people to move away from the area. Kate didn't need to be told twice. "Can we—?" she began to ask.

"Follow me," he said, holding out his hand to her. Leaving her hot chocolate behind, Kate held on, and Luca took the lead, winding in and out of the frantic crowd until they found their way out of the square. Once clear, they crossed the bridge and kept walking until they eventually found themselves in the park.

"I think we'll be safe here," Luca said.

"Are you sure?" Kate asked. She wasn't interested in taking any chances with swans running amok. She'd had enough experience with large fowl to know they were not animals she wanted to tangle with. And she'd heard horror stories. A shiver ran through her at the thought.

"Don't worry. I'll protect you." His warm smile was somewhat reassuring.

She realized suddenly that she was still holding his hand. Luca seemed to notice too and was staring thoughtfully at their entwined fingers.

It was crazy. She knew it was. There was no future with Luca, but in that moment she didn't care. The present was gift enough.

The park was full of ice sculptures. Luca explained that artists come from all over the world to participate in the ice carving contest as part of the holiday festival. They wandered through the maze of sculptures, hand-in-hand, marveling at the work that had been done. Some were quite elaborate displays that must have taken weeks to get just right. Kate was in awe of the designs, though her favorite was the princess in the flowing gown, dancing with her prince on a cloud of snow.

"Do you want to head back?" Luca asked after they'd spent an hour admiring the displays. "I know the animal sanctuary people had a booth at the carnival, so they likely have the swan situation under control by now."

Afternoon faded to evening. Kate caught only a few glimpses of Mrs. Hall here and there, so she was surprised when the text came through saying that Mrs. Hall was going to ride back to the resort with some friends and Kate should stay and enjoy the carnival.

Luca had stepped away to take a call from the resort, so Kate found an empty bench and sat down to wait for him. It was strange how peaceful it seemed here even with the bustle of the carnival crowd around her. She glanced around, looking for anyone she recognized.

Cleo was there, standing with a group of friends. Kate

wasn't sure if Cleo would remember her, but she waved anyway when she caught Cleo's eye. Cleo smiled.

That's when Kate noticed. Right over Cleo's head. Mistletoe.

Kate traced the path of the wires hanging all around the town square and suddenly realized… There was mistletoe everywhere. It was a veritable minefield of mistletoe. A surge of fear raced up her spine, and she cautiously lifted her chin to peek above her own head.

Oh. Sweet. Lord.

"So, what did I miss?" Luca asked, flopping onto the bench beside her holding two cups of hot tea.

"Nothing." It came out as a squeak. Kate cleared her throat and tried again. "Nothing." Much better.

"Jake is here," Luca said, offering her one of the cups.

"Well, that's fantastic news," she said. She took the cup and held it with both hands, trying to absorb the warmth into her freezing fingers. Somehow she'd have to find a way to move them away from the mistletoe before Luca saw it.

Kate liked him. That wasn't in dispute. And she hadn't stopped thinking about his kiss all day. But she didn't want him to think she was angling for a repeat performance. Not when they'd come to an understanding about where they stood. It wouldn't be fair to either of them.

She scanned the square to see where Jake might be. The farther away, the better.

Then she saw him. Naturally, Jake had wasted no time discovering the mistletoe grid and was making his way around the square, one mistletoe at a time.

"Is he—?" Luca asked, squinting to see better.

"Drunk?" Kate finished. She traced his uneven

movements around the square. "I mean, it could be his pain meds, but… yeah, I'm gonna go with yes on that one."

For several minutes, Kate and Luca sat quietly watching Jake. They couldn't help themselves. It was like watching a train wreck.

He would see a woman, saunter in her direction as if he wasn't on a mission, *accidentally* bump into her, apologize profusely while angling her to the side where he knew the mistletoe hung. When in the exact position, he'd glance up and say, *Would you look at that*, flash his predatory grin, and go in for the payoff.

Maybe if he hadn't been so drunk, he might have scored some digits from one or two of his conquests, but he was clearly inebriated, so instead, he was slapped.

Every.

Single.

Time.

Kate thought that eventually Jake would give up and skulk off with his wounded pride. But he never did, and the onslaught lasted longer than Kate was willing to watch.

Luca must have felt the same way. With a look of horror on his face, he turned to her and asked, "Do you want to—"

"Yes, please!" She almost shouted it. *Anywhere* would be better than here.

Unfortunately, the shout caught Jake's attention, who had been steadily working his way closer and closer to where Luca and Kate had been sitting.

"Kate!" he yelled and stumbled toward them.

She wouldn't have thought he could move that fast in his current state, but there he was. Right beside her. Before she could escape.

"So, this is where you've been hiding all day," he said, slurring ever so slightly. "I've been looking for you, you know." His head wobbled, and he cast a glance above Kate's head, then a slow, disturbing sneer spread across his lips, and his gaze dropped to Kate's mouth. "Oh, ho-ho! Look who's under the mistletoe!"

Jake leaned toward her, and she knew what was coming, but she was like a deer in the headlights—unable to move, unable to make it stop.

When Luca's hand came between them and pushed against Jake's chest effectively blocking Jake's forward motion, it took a moment for Kate to realize what was happening. Jake stumbled backward and landed in the lap of a rather large man, spilling the poor guy's hot chocolate everywhere.

The man's face turned bright red, and Kate could tell Jake was about to meet with the wrath of a man deprived of his hot chocolate.

She probably would have been content to witness that.

But she was standing under the mistletoe.

Luca took her hand and turned her to face him. He shot a meaningful glance at the sprig of white berries above their heads and smiled as his gaze returned to her face. "Oh, ho-ho," he whispered as he stepped closer. "Look who's under the mistletoe."

A warm thrill shot through her, and she focused on his lips in anticipation.

Luca took her face in his hands and kissed her.

CHAPTER NINE
Heedless of the Wind and Weather

THE NEXT DAY WAS A TORRENT of business. Mrs. Hall seemed to feel that the previous two days of relaxing and festivities had been an exercise in procrastination, which she could not afford.

Her first text blasted in at 5:05 AM, demanding Kate's attention from that moment until she fell exhausted into her bed just after midnight.

Luca had also been kept busy with preparations for the Christmas Eve festivities. She saw him once as she passed through the lobby. He smiled, and that one gesture got her through the rest of the day.

When her phone chirped just after she had crawled into bed, she considered throwing it against the wall, but changed her mind when she saw the notification was from

Luca.

LUCA: HOW WAS YOUR DAY?

Kate responded with a yawning emoji.

LUCA: MINE TOO. WHAT'S ON THE AGENDA FOR TOMORROW?

ME: I GET TO PICK UP MRS. HALL'S DRESS FROM MRS. STRADLEY.

LUCA: THAT'S EXCITING! ARE YOU EXCITED?

ME: I'M NERVOUS. WHAT IF SHE DOESN'T LIKE IT?

LUCA: I'VE SEEN YOUR DESIGN. SHE'LL LOVE IT. SHE LIVES FOR FASHION, REMEMBER?

ME: I GUESS. I'M STILL NERVOUS. I'VE SEEN WHAT SHE CAN DO WHEN SHE DOESN'T LIKE SOMETHING.

LUCA: YOU HAVE NOTHING TO WORRY ABOUT. IT'S GOING TO BE BEAUTIFUL. IF SHE'S WORTH ANYTHING AS A DESIGNER, SHE'LL LOVE IT.

ME: THANK YOU

Kate added a heart emoji, then thought better of it and replaced it with a bashful smile emoji.

LUCA: SO… YOU HUNGRY FOR AN OMELET?

Kate wanted to see him, but her body told a different story. The last few days had taken their toll on her, and there was no way she was getting out of that bed.

ME: I'M SO TIRED. RAIN CHECK?

Luca sent an emoji with big sad eyes, then followed it up with another text.

LUCA: I UNDERSTAND. I DON'T LIKE IT, BUT I UNDERSTAND. MAYBE TOMORROW NIGHT?

ME: DO YOU HAVE A BUSY DAY PLANNED?

LUCA: JUST MORE CHRISTMAS EVE STUFF. I COULD PROBABLY MEET YOU FOR LUNCH IF YOU CAN GET AWAY.

ME: THAT SOUNDS GOOD. I'LL TEXT YOU AFTER I'M DONE

AT MRS. STRADLEY'S.

LUCA: OKAY, I'LL BE LOOKING FORWARD TO IT. SWEET DREAMS.

ME: YOU TOO

Kate's thumb hovered over the heart emoji for a long moment. No. Too soon. She lay her phone on the nightstand and rolled over. How long had it been since Kate had had a normal texting conversation just because? She couldn't even remember the last time she had used her phone for anything but business. She closed her eyes and smiled, savoring the memory of Luca's kiss on her lips.

Yes, tomorrow was an important day. It would either bring Kate a huge step closer to becoming the designer she'd been working toward her whole life, or it would crush her dreams. But for some reason, the thought of time with Luca soothed her fears, and she couldn't wait to see him.

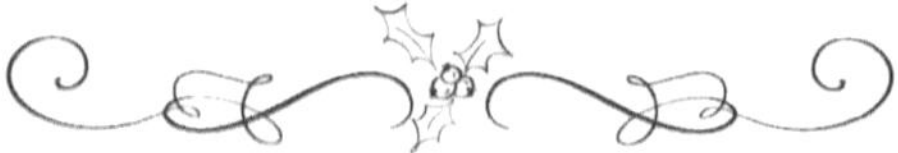

"OH, MRS. STRADLEY! IT'S beautiful! Exactly what I pictured!" Kate exclaimed.

"Well, it was your design, Kate. You have so much talent. I honestly can't believe Ms. Skye-Adams hasn't already snapped you up for her design team."

Heat creeped into Kate's cheeks, and she knew she was blushing, but she tried to push it away. She had created an amazing design. Mrs. Hall would have to be blind not to notice. And if she was going to make a go of a design career, she'd have to learn to take compliments without turning the shade of a ripe tomato.

"Thank you so much, Mrs. Stradley. You do amazing work." She tucked the gold gown back into the garment bag and hung it on the hook beside her.

Mrs. Stradley's lips curled into a sly smile. "Do you want to see the other one?"

"The other one?" Kate could feel her jaw drop. "You— you finished already?"

"Oh yes. Cleo is a special favorite of mine. I worked through the night on this one."

"She doesn't know, does she?"

Mrs. Stradley shook her head vehemently and tapped her forefinger to her lips. "No, no. Mum was the word." She winked conspiratorially, then quirked an eyebrow. "Though I will say she was rather upset when she returned to buy that gown and it had already been sold. I got to hear all about it at the animal sanctuary when she got back. Something about being the redheaded stepchild of Huckleberry Falls… There were tears. It would've broken my heart if I hadn't known what was in store for her. Wait here. I'll grab it." She tapped Kate lightly on the arm and disappeared into the hallway, returning a moment later with another garment bag.

Kate took the bag from her and held it up while Mrs. Stradley opened it to reveal the glacier blue gown. She slipped the hanger out of the bag and held it up for Kate's inspection.

The breath caught in Kate's throat. And her hands flew, of their own will, to her mouth. It was the most beautiful thing she'd ever seen. A tear burned behind her eyes, threatening to spill over. Mrs. Stradley had taken her vision and made it reality, and the result was better than even *she* had imagined.

There were no words.

"What do you think?"

"Oh…" Kate squeaked, then in barely a whisper, "Oh, Mrs. Stradley, it's—" Then the tears did push through her carefully crafted defenses and slip down her cheeks. "It's the most beautiful thing." She was afraid to meet Mrs. Stradley's gaze then. She didn't want her to see her crying over a dress, but when she finally did look up, Mrs. Stradley was crying too.

"Do you think Cleo will like it?"

Mrs. Stradley laid one hand on Kate's arm. "She will love it, Kate. And I am certain… there *will* be tears." She tucked the dress back into its bag and handed it to Kate. Then she tugged the handkerchief out of her sleeve and dabbed at her own eyes. "So many tears."

"Where can I find her, do you think?"

"She's probably at the animal sanctuary right now. That's where she spends most of her time, so that's where I'd begin," Mrs. Stradley said.

Kate didn't remember seeing an animal sanctuary in town. "How do I get there from here?"

"I wouldn't go on foot. Not with the wind blowing like this. Did you drive or take the shuttle?"

"I rode in on the shuttle."

"You know what?" Mrs. Stradley patted Kate's arm. "I want to see the look on Cleo's face when she sees that gown. What if I tag along? I'll drive."

"Of course! I would love for you to be there!"

"I'll grab my coat."

IT WAS JUST BEFORE lunch when Kate and Mrs. Stradley pulled into the parking lot at the animal sanctuary.

Kate sent a quick text to Luca to let him know they were dropping off Cleo's dress and what time she'd be able to meet, and then she and Mrs. Stradley headed inside to find Cleo.

The jingle of the bell on the door announced their arrival, and the woman behind the desk looked up as they walked in.

"Good morning, Red," Mrs. Stradley said, smiling.

"Good morning, Mrs. Stradley. I didn't think you were coming in today."

"Oh, I'm not here. I'm actually just looking for Cleo. Is she around?"

"Yeah, she's here somewhere. Probably hiding." Red laughed at what appeared to be a private joke.

"Who can blame her after the week she's had?" Mrs. Stradley said and chuckled along with her.

Red seemed to notice Kate for the first time. She stood and walked around the desk to meet her. "Hi, I'm Charlotte. But everyone calls me Red." She tugged on her long red hair as if to explain the nickname.

"I'm so sorry," Mrs. Stradley said, seeming to remember suddenly that she had brought a guest. "Red, this is Kate Curtis. She's the designer from New York I was telling you about. She's here for the holidays, staying at the resort."

Mrs. Stradley's description of Kate caught her off-guard. She glanced at Mrs. Stradley's face, searching for a sign of irony. No one had ever introduced her as a designer before, but Mrs. Stradley seemed completely oblivious to her slip-up.

"It's so nice to meet you, Kate," "Red said and offered her hand in greeting.

"It's nice to meet you too, Red."

"How do you like Huckleberry Falls? It's a far cry from New York City, I bet."

Kate couldn't help but smile. The town was lovely, but there was one particular part of it that she was especially fond of. And at that moment he was driving down the hill to meet her.

"I love it," she said. "It's so peaceful and beautiful."

"I'll give you the beautiful, but I could tell you stories that will make you think better of the peaceful," Red said, laughing again, and Mrs. Stradley raised both eyebrows and nodded her full agreement.

"Not for the animal sanctuary, that's for sure!"

"Oh! Were you the ones who corralled the wild swans at the carnival?"

"Let me tell you, Kate, if the swans were the only animals we've dealt with this week, it would have been more than enough," Mrs. Stradley said.

Red pointed at the garment bag hanging over Kate's arm. Her voice lowered to a whisper. "Is that it?" She was asking Mrs. Stradley.

"Yes." Mrs. Stradley glanced around the room as if making sure they were alone. "Do you want to see it?"

"Do geese fly south for winter?"

"You'd better hope so. If we have to rescue any more large waterfowl around here, I'm quitting and moving to the city." Mrs. Stradley reached for the garment bag and held it up for Kate to unzip.

Kate slipped the gown out of the bag and held it up for Red's inspection.

"You and me bo— Oh my word! That's the most beautiful thing I've ever seen!" Red took a step back, admiring the gown with wide eyes. "She doesn't know?"

"Nope."

"Can I watch you give it to her?"

Kate returned the dress to the bag and zipped it up.

"Of course. Should we call her in?" Mrs. Stradley looked at Kate. "You ready?"

Kate nodded. But her stomach was doing flip-flops.

Red picked up a walkie talkie from her desk and spoke into it. "Cleo?"

There was static for several seconds, so Red tried again. "Cleo, are you there?"

More static, then, "Hey, Red, what's up?"

"We need you in the office right away. Can you come?"

"Sure. Give me two minutes."

Mrs. Stradley put her arm around Kate's shoulders. "Don't you worry, hon. The dress is gorgeous. She's going to love it."

Kate could only nod in response. The dress was beautiful. Everything was going to be fine. If she was completely honest, it was the thought of unveiling Mrs. Hall's gown that was really worrying her. That was the do-or-die.

The rattle of a door closing down the hall caught her attention, and within seconds Cleo came striding into the office out of breath like she'd just run a 5K.

"I'm here! What's the emergency?" Her forehead was creased with concern, then she noticed Kate. "Kate, right?" Her concern seemed to vanish in the wake of her friendly smile.

"Yes, that's right. How are you, Cleo?"

Cleo shrugged. "I would say *I can't complain*, but I feel like that would be inviting chaos."

Mrs. Stradley and Red exchanged a cryptic look. Then Mrs. Stradley said, "Kate brought something for you, Cleo." All eyes turned to Kate.

"Um, yes, if you don't like it, it's okay, but after I met you the other day, I had some ideas for your dress."

Cleo frowned and shook her head. "Oh, Kate, I'm sorry. Someone else bought that gown you helped me find. I don't have it."

"No, that's not what I... I mean, yes, I know someone bought it. I did." She held the garment bag out for Cleo. "Here."

Cleo's eyes narrowed in confusion. "You bought it? Why would you—"

"Oh, for Pete's sake, Cleo," Mrs Stradley said. She pulled the zipper down on the garment bag and slipped the gown out, holding it up high so Cleo could see it. "Kate bought the dress and redesigned it... for *you!*"

Cleo's eyes grew wide in shock. "For me?" Her gaze took in the whole gown, then cautiously, she lifted her hand to touch the sheer frosted-blue tulle. "Really?" She looked at Kate.

Kate nodded.

With both hands, Cleo covered her mouth in disbelief. Tears filled her eyes. Staring at the gown, she could only shake her head and mutter in a voice barely above a whisper, "It's the most beautiful— I never dreamed of anything so beautiful! It's perfect…" Her eyes met Kate's. "It's perfect. Thank you. Thank you so so much." The tears streamed down her face, and Kate could feel the burn of unwelcome tears behind her own eyes as well.

She glanced at Mrs. Stradley, who seemed on the verge of an old-fashioned ugly cry. Red wasn't far behind. And nobody could see to pass out the tissues.

LUCA WAITED FOR KATE outside Dan's diner. He had been looking forward to this part of his day all morning. Even with the stress of the preparations for both the community Christmas ball and the traditional Christmas Eve dinner party at the resort, he hadn't been able to keep his mind off Kate. Now, as she bounced down the sidewalk toward him practically glowing, he tried to convince himself the feeling in the pit of his stomach was just hunger.

Her eyes lit up when she saw him, and he could be wrong, but his heart might have skipped a beat when she started toward him in a full sprint, stopping just short of leaping into his arms. She bounced lightly on her feet.

"Hi!" she said, beaming the brightest smile he'd seen all day.

A smile meant only for him.

"Hi," he whispered. Her face was just inches away. Would it be wrong to take her in his arms and kiss her right here on the street in front of God and everybody?

Probably.

Luca swallowed hard.

Breathe in. Breathe out.

He cleared his throat.

"So how did it go with Cleo?" he asked, finally.

"So good! We all cried. Here..." She pulled her phone out of her coat pocket and navigated to her photos. "Look how beautiful she is!" Her eyes sparkled like emeralds catching the sun.

You are beautiful.

Kate held up her phone to show him.

She was right. The dress was beautiful, and Cleo looked beautiful in it. "She really does," he said. "Your design is perfect for her!" *And you are perfect.* He knew better than to say it out loud. Kate would be leaving in a matter of a few short days. It wouldn't be fair to either of them if they got too involved. Too attached.

Deep down, though, he knew it was already too late.

"So, lunch?" He lifted a hand toward the diner. "Dan's is the best in town."

Kate quirked an eyebrow like she didn't quite believe him.

"It probably won't kill you," he said with a smile.

KATE'S GRIN FELT LIKE it was permanently etched into her face. She was certain she must look like The Joker as she strode through the corridor on the way to Mrs. Hall's suite. Today was her favorite day.

The new-found confidence resounded in her knock on

the door. She could hear faint voices from behind the door, then it opened slowly. Jake peered at her in such an odd way, she hesitated, second guessing the confidence she'd had just a moment before.

"Come in, Kate, come in. Don't stand in the doorway like a security system salesman," Mrs. Hall said, waving her hand dismissively. She lounged on the settee, sipping a glass of red wine.

Kate stepped over the threshold, past Jake, and he closed the door behind her. He looked a little paler than usual. She couldn't resist a knowing smile and made a mental note to congratulate Bernard, the pillow chocolate guy, on a job well done.

"What did you bring me?" Mrs. Hall nodded at the garment bag draped over Kate's arm.

The question drew Kate back to her task at hand. A flutter of butterflies danced in her stomach at the thought of presenting the gown to Mrs. Hall. She tried to suppress them. After all, Mrs. Stradley had taken Kate's vision for the gown to a higher plane, and after the success with Cleo's gown earlier that day, she was convinced that even Mrs. Hall would be pleased. She drew in a deep breath and let it slowly release.

"Kate?"

"Yes. This is your gown for the Christmas ball." She strode toward the settee, holding up the garment bag by the hanger, preparing to unzip it.

"Where did you get it?"

"I picked it up at a local shop the other day, and then—"

"No."

"—I hired a— what?" She couldn't have said what it sounded like she said. Mrs. Hall loved to look at gowns by any designer. She would never just reject it off the cuff. Without even looking at it. Would she?

"No."

"No?"

"Really, Kate, don't be exhausting." Mrs. Hall took another slow sip from her glass and pinched the bridge of her nose as if she were fighting a headache. "You know better than anyone, I would think, that Cynthia Skye-Adams cannot be caught wearing something off the rack of a local shop. No matter how upscale its clientele. It won't happen."

"Mrs. Hall, I think if you just look at the dress—"

"No."

"No?"

"Is there an echo in here?" Jake sat down in the chair across from his mother and offered Kate a snide smirk.

Kate glared at him.

"Ooo… death glare."

"Oh, shut up, Jake," his mother interjected.

"You won't even look at it? It's really beautiful, I think you'll be pleased."

"Kate…" Mrs. Hall took a long, slow sip of her wine, and then settled her gaze on Kate. "I'm sure you spent time scouring the racks for the dress you thought I'd least despise, and I'm sure you feel you have found the perfect gown. But I'm telling you now — and this will be the last word on it — and I will say it slowly, so it can sink all the way in… I. Will. *Not.* Wear. That. Gown. Put it out of your mind."

She set her glass on the end table, stood to her feet, and held out her hand toward Jake.

"Hand me my phone. I'll have Paige overnight me

something from my Christmas line."

Kate's heart fell into her stomach, crushing the butterflies that had been there only a moment before. "I can do that for you, Mrs. Hall," she said, but her voice lacked spirit, and Mrs. Hall only rolled her eyes.

"I will handle this myself, Kate. If you had done your job in the first place, we wouldn't even be having this discussion. Clearly, it requires my *personal* touch." She tapped on her phone and pulled off her clip-on earring before nestling the phone to her ear. "You should go on to bed, Kate. You look exhausted. We'll need you fresh in the morning. Be here at 8:00 — Paige? Drop everything, I have a priority one assignment for you."

Kate turned to go, taking her garment bag and crushed spirit with her.

"Want me to tuck you in?" Jake asked, waggling his eyebrows suggestively.

"Jake," Kate said. "You look a little pale. I hear dark chocolate is good for that kind of thing." Then she strode to the door and left without another word.

CHAPTER TEN
Fill the Meadcup, Drain the Barrel

WHEN THE ELEVATOR DOOR SLID CLOSED behind her, Kate slumped to the floor against the wall of the elevator and let the tears fall. It had seemed so perfect, the plan to get Mrs. Hall to recognize her talent. Foolproof even. But she wouldn't even look at the dress. Wouldn't hear Kate out before rejecting her.

And now she was back to square one.

There was no hope. It was never going to happen for her.

The bell chimed and the door slid open to the basement. Kate didn't move. She just sat there with her face buried in her hands.

"Kate?" Luca's voice surprised her. "Kate, are you okay? What happened?" He swept in and dropped to his knees beside her. "What is it? Did someone hurt you?" The fear in his voice was evident. He grabbed her arms, and she lifted her face.

She was a hot mess. She knew it. Probably had mascara everywhere, but she didn't care. Her dream was dead, and right then, she was just struggling to keep her head above the flood of despair her life had become.

"What's wrong? Tell me," Luca said. His eyes pleaded with her to answer.

Kate shook her head. "She wouldn't even look at it." A fresh wave of tears filled her eyes, blurring her vision.

"Oh, Kate, I'm so sorry." He slid into place beside her and wrapped his arms around her.

Kate allowed herself to lean into his embrace, letting his warmth envelop her.

The doors slid closed again.

They sat there in silence for several minutes until Kate felt like she could breathe again.

"There's an author staying in the resort this weekend," Luca said, offhandedly.

"Oh yeah?" Kate said, dabbing at her eyes with her sleeve. That was a random piece of information. "Who is it?"

"Promise you won't tell anyone?"

She nodded, still confused about why he was bringing it up.

"Wendy Knight."

"That's cool." Was he just trying to distract her? Interesting strategy.

"Well, I was thinking," Luca began, a sly smile curling his lips, "I bet if we explained the situation, she'd write Mrs. Hall into a book and kill her off for you."

Kate snorted in laughter. Immediately, she covered her face with her hands. So embarrassing.

Luca laughed. "Was that a snort?"

She shook her head. Still hiding her face. "No!"

"I mean, I'd send Bernard, but people like that are usually so constipated from the rectal-cranial inversion, the special chocolates are just a relief to them."

"Stop! Oh, stop!" She laughed, dropping her hands but trying desperately to keep herself from snorting again.

"What time do you have to meet her tomorrow?"

"Eight. But I don't think I can face her."

Luca still had his arm around her shoulders, and he was slowly rubbing her forearm with the other hand.

Kate closed her eyes and rested her head on his shoulder. She felt completely safe and understood here in his arms. Like nowhere else in her world.

"Did you say she didn't even look at it?" He slipped his arm off her shoulders and took her hand.

Kate nodded and sniffed, staring at their entwined fingers. "She wouldn't even let me take it out of the bag. Which is really unlike her. I've never known her to refuse to even look. It's weird."

"Well, if she hasn't seen it yet, there's still hope. The key is presentation. In a place where she has no other option but to see it." He stood suddenly, pulling her up with him. "Come on, I have an idea." He pressed the button and the elevator doors slid open.

LUCA STOOD AT THE front entrance, eyeing the storm clouds gathered over the resort. It was going to be one of those days; he could feel it.

As if on cue, the elevator doors on the other side of the lobby slid open, and Mrs. Hall appeared with the look of someone on the rampage. The click of her heels on the wood floor echoed in his ears and sent a chill down his spine. He followed her path to the front desk where she slapped her hand on the counter to demand Renate's attention.

Renate, ever the sweet and patient soul, put down the schedule she was working on and approached Mrs. Hall with a gentle smile. "*Bonjour*, Madame Hall, how may I help you this morning?"

"I need to know what room my assistant—Kate Curtis—is staying in."

Luca's ears perked up.

"I'm sorry, madame, I'm not allowed to give out that information. The privacy of our guests is—"

"Nonsense. I am paying for that room, and I demand to know."

Renate cast a glance to Luca across the room, meeting his gaze. He nodded and moved toward them.

"I understand, Madame Hall," Renate said. "Have you tried calling her?"

"What kind of question is that?" Mrs. Hall's voice lowered, as if to hide her aggravation from onlookers. "Why would I be down here with you if I hadn't already exhausted all other means of contacting her?"

"Is everything all right here?" Luca asked as he stepped in beside Mrs. Hall.

She glanced at him, and the anger flashing there

caused him to take a step back. "Luca, isn't it? Aren't you in charge here?"

"I'm one of the managers. Is there anything I can help you with, madame?"

"I need to see Kate. This *woman...*" The word dripped off her tongue like acid. "...refuses to give me information that is on my own account although I am rightfully entitled to know it."

"What is it that you want to know?"

"Her room."

Luca turned to the computer and pretended to look up the information Mrs. Hall was asking for. "Oh, I see that she is housed in the staff area. I can give you her room number, but it will do you no good. The area is off-limits to guests."

"Ridiculous! I have to see Kate right away. She isn't answering her cell phone, and I have no way to contact her."

That news sent a shot of concern through him. Kate had been upset the previous night, but when he left her at her room, she seemed to be doing much better. They had discussed his idea and she had said it was good. What had changed?

"Perhaps if we call her room?" He picked up the phone and dialed her extension. It rang several times, but Kate didn't answer. Mrs. Hall glared at him with impatient expectation.

Renate nudged him lightly with her elbow, and when he looked at her, he traced her gaze to the entrance of the hall leading to the service elevator. Kate was peering around the corner at him. He frowned and shook his head slightly, then cast a glance toward Mrs. Hall, hoping Kate would understand his meaning without drawing the attention of Mrs. Hall, but when he glanced back toward the hall, Kate was gone.

He returned the phone to the cradle, shaking his head. "I'm sorry, madame. She isn't answering."

"Then I want you to go check on her." Mrs. Hall glowered straight into his eyes, directing the full force of her intimidating stare on him.

"I can do that for you, madame, of course. Is there anything in particular you'd like me to say? A message perhaps?"

"I prefer to give my messages in person, Luca. Just make sure she's still alive and tell her to answer her phone! I am *not*—" Her voice had raised several levels in volume, and she seemed to realize it, glancing behind her and lowering to a whisper as she turned to face him again and said through her teeth, "—inclined to play nursemaid to the sick."

"I'll do that right away," he said. "Will you wait here, or shall I ring your room when I have news?"

"I will assume that if I hear from Kate, you will have done what I've asked. If I hear from *you* at all, I will be very disappointed in the service at this resort."

She spun on her heel and charged back the way she had come.

Renate released the breath she had apparently been holding. "I believe that means she won't be waiting here."

"Did you see which way she went?" Luca asked as he strode toward the corridor Kate had been in only a moment before.

"No, I think maybe she ducked back into the elevator. I'll check the back hall. Are you checking downstairs?"

"Yes." That was all he had time to say. He ducked into the corridor and sprinted for the elevator.

Outside Kate's door, he listened for a brief moment before knocking.

"Kate?" He waited for a response. "It's Luca. Everything okay?"

He heard a crash on the other side of the door and a string of curse words, then, "Hang on, I'm coming." More unsettling thumps, and then the latch rattled in the door, and it opened suddenly.

Kate peeked out, glancing to the right and left of Luca, probably checking to see if he was alone. Her eyes settled on him. "Hi," she whispered.

"Hi." He couldn't help the smile that leapt to his face. Kate was okay. Luca leaned closer to study her face for signs of trouble. "Are you doing alright?"

She closed one eye in a prolonged wink, then raised a finger to her lips as if about to tell him a secret. "I'm fine, but… I might be… a little bit drunk." She exhaled the proof into his face.

Rum.

"Got into the eggnog, did you?"

She held up her finger and thumb about an inch apart. "Just a bit."

"It's nine o'clock in the morning."

"It wasn't when I started." She laughed and swung the door open giving Luca space to enter.

He stepped past her and surveyed the room, spotting the pile of tiny glass bottles empty on the coffee table. "How much have you had?"

Kate held onto the wall for support. "Um… I don't exactly know. I lost count." She seemed to look off into the distance. "Count. Count. That's a weird word. Count… Count Drac-u-la…" She laughed at the words rolling off her tongue.

"I thought you were feeling better. We had a plan." Luca reached for her arm to help her to the couch.

"I know. I'm sorry. I just… I just couldn't face her. Not after last night. I just needed some time to process. You know?" She stumbled, falling forward. Luca caught her, and she gazed hazily into his eyes with her arms draped around his shoulders.

"You have the sexiest smile I've ever seen." She gazed intently at him. "And your accent—your accent makes my knees weak." She stared at him a second as if deep in thought, then closed one eye and wrinkled up her nose. "Did I just say that out loud?"

He lifted her into his arms, carried her to the couch, and set her down gently. "I'm going to make you some coffee."

"Mm, coffee. Can it be Irish?"

"Uh, no. I think you've had enough, don't you?" His cell phone buzzed, and he saw a notification from Renate. He reached for the phone on the end table and dialed the front desk.

"It's Luca."

"Did you find Ms. Curtis?" Renate asked.

"Yes. She's okay, but she's not in any condition to see anyone."

"What will you tell Madame Hall?"

"I don't know yet. I'll think of something."

"Okay, keep me posted."

Luca hung up and looked at Kate who was smiling dreamily up at him.

Coffee. He strode to the kitchenette and started brewing a full pot.

"Here. Drink this." He handed her a cup of the steaming liquid and sat down next to her.

She lifted it to her lips tentatively, testing the temperature. A practice he had noticed before. She cringed when it burned her lips but sipped at it anyway.

"I have a confession to make," Kate said, after swallowing the dregs of her second cup of coffee and holding it up for a refill. *It's a Wonderful Life* played on the television, and the two of them were sitting shoulder to shoulder, wrapped up in a fuzzy blanket.

"Yeah? What's that?" Luca asked. He filled her cup the third time.

"When I was a little girl, I thought *Deck the Halls* was about knocking down the walls to make a deck."

Luca chuckled at the revelation.

"Whenever I hear it now, I just imagine punching Mrs. Hall in the face." She took a long sip from her mug, licked her full lips, and said, "It's my favorite song."

The mischievous twinkle in her eye amused him and he laughed.

"I can understand that sentiment."

She cocked her head and seemed to study him for a long moment, then blurted, "You wanna know something else?" Her speech was clearing up and the coffee seemed to be having the desired effect. It was probably time to get her a little breakfast.

"Of course."

"You're the first guy who's kissed me since I was in high school." She leaned her head against his shoulder and closed her eyes. She sighed contentedly. "I can't stop thinking about your lips."

That was the rum talking, he knew, and though every part of him wanted to reciprocate the confession, he also knew he couldn't take advantage of the situation, not like this. The realization hit him all at once.

Kate wasn't just another girl. She was special to him. Important. He never wanted to do anything to hurt her. And he didn't want to lose her, but he would do whatever it took to make sure her dream was achieved, even though it would mean there would be no possibility that she could stay.

"I'm going to go get you some breakfast. Will you be okay here for a few minutes?" He stood and waited for her answer which came in the form of her soft, even breaths. Luca slipped the coffee cup out of her hands, spread the blanket over her, and propped a pillow beside her to keep her from tipping over, then he leaned close and pressed a gentle kiss to her forehead.

"Everything's going to be okay," he whispered, then he left.

WHEN KATE AWOKE, THE light filtering in from the bathroom seemed to sear her brain, and she shielded her eyes. There were two bottles of water sitting on the coffee table in front of her. A scribbled note on a sheet of the resort letterhead lay beside them.

Kate, hope you're feeling better. I left some water for you. Drink it. I'm going to hold Mrs. Hall off as long as possible, but you might want to text her as soon as you're ready to face the wrath. She's on the warpath. I'll be back to check on you around dinner time.

Luca

A knock sounded on the door, sounding a little too much like a sledgehammer slamming onto her skull. She covered her ears and stood clumsily to her feet, then stumbled toward the door.

"Who is it?" she whispered hoarsely. Her mouth was like sand. She glanced back at the water waiting on the table. There was a vague recollection of there being a pile of tiny alcohol bottles there earlier. The pounding on the door rocked her brain, and she dove for the latch, to open it before whoever it was made her head explode.

It wasn't latched though. Odd. She opened the door a crack and peered into the hall. It was Luca.

"Hi," he whispered. "Can I come in?"

Kate hesitated a minute. Luca had been here earlier. The memory was foggy, but it was there.

"Sure." She opened the door and let him through.

"How are you feeling?" He still whispered. That was a mercy anyway. "Have you had any water?" He was carrying a tray from the kitchen. The smell made her stomach turn.

"I..." she began, but when her gravelly voice ricocheted off the insides of her skull, she thought better of it and carefully shook her head.

Luca set the tray on the coffee table. He opened one of the water bottles and handed it to her. "Trust me."

She drank it slowly at first, then finished it off. He handed her the second bottle. Kate took her place on the couch, resting her head against the back. She didn't remember ever feeling so miserable. That was probably why she rarely drank much.

"So…" Luca leaned against the kitchen counter and folded his arms over his chest. "Do you want to talk about it?"

"There's nothing to talk about really. I mean, clearly, I shouldn't be indulging in Christmas cheer."

He chuckled and shook his head. "I think the Christmas cheer is alright, but you might want to avoid the rum." He lifted a hand to gesture at the seat beside her. "May I?"

"Sure." Something was familiar about having him beside her on the couch. "Um… did I say anything weird before?"

"You were really enamored with the word *count*," he said, smiling at her.

"Oh, geez."

"To be fair, it is an interesting word. Count. Count. Count Drac-u-la." Luca snickered.

Kate swatted at him. "Stop!" Too loud, too soon. "Shh!" More to herself, as she cringed from the stabbing pain in her head. Having her words echoed back at her seemed to strike a chord in her memory, and she closed her eyes in embarrassment, cringing inwardly. Another very good reason to never indulge again.

She opened an eye to peek at him. He was staring at her oddly.

She was almost afraid to ask. "There's more, isn't there?"

"You really like my sexy smile." Luca flashed it again, as if to rub it in. "And my accent makes your—"

"My knees weak… oh my word." Kate buried her face

in her hands. She couldn't bear to look at him.

"Ah, so it's true," he whispered, nudging her arm with his. "Don't worry, I won't tell anyone how smitten you are with me. However, I do have a confession of my own to make..." Luca reached for her hands and peeled them away from her face, turning her toward him.

"What's that?" she asked, cringing at what might be coming. Something told her she had said something even more humiliating, and she wasn't anxious to be reminded of it.

His gaze dropped to her mouth.

"I can't stop thinking about your lips either." And before his words registered in her brain, his lips crushed to hers, halting any further thought.

CHAPTER ELEVEN
Don We Now Our Gay Apparel

"I HOPE YOU'RE HAPPY, KATE," MRS. HALL said the moment she opened the door that morning. "When you called in sick yesterday, I had to use one of the resort's bunglers to get everything done, and he was miserably inadequate."

"Sorry about that, Mrs. Hall."

Mrs. Hall examined her closely. "I don't think you are, but never mind. I just don't want it to happen again. What was wrong with you anyway? The fools downstairs just kept saying you were ordered to rest by the on-staff doctor."

"She was probably sleeping off a bender," Jake said. "You know how all these working-class people cover for each other." He was sitting across the room, eating a scone, and looking rather glassy-eyed himself.

Kate studied him. What did he know about it?

"Stop talking through your hat, Jake," his mother said, rolling her eyes. "Our Kate is not one of them." She turned back to Kate. "Never mind. Let's just get our day organized. The Christmas ball is this evening in the village." She pointed at the window. "Naturally, it's snowing, so there's nothing else to do but prepare for the ball.

"My gown is hanging in the other room. I'll need you to make sure it is in pristine condition. I had Paige send one over for you as well, Kate, so do what you need to do in order to be ready. What time does the ball start? We'll need to reserve a car."

Kate pulled up the schedule on her phone. "It says here they will have a caravan of luxury SUVs to transport the guests. Caravan leaves at six o'clock sharp. I can put you on the reservation list if you'd like."

"Yes, do that right away."

"I'll grab the gowns and take care of the reservation and the dresses at the same time."

"Ah!" Mrs. Hall sighed in mock relief. "Efficiency at last."

Jake started to laugh but was immediately silenced by Mrs. Hall's death glare.

Kate retrieved the two gowns and left.

Once in the lobby, Kate looked for Luca.

"So how did it go?" Luca asked, coming up behind her. His closeness sent a thrill through her, reviving the memory of the evening before.

Kate turned to look at him. "Well, I didn't kill her."

"That's a relief," Luca said. "Cleaning up after a

murder is my second least favorite part of this job."

"That's exactly why I refrained. I knew you already had enough to do, and I wanted to save you the trouble."

"So thoughtful," he said. "I like that about you."

"I do what I can."

"What do you have here?" He tapped on the garment bags.

"Mrs. Hall's dress for the ball." She cast a sidelong glance at him as they walked together. "And one for me. Are you—are you planning to attend tonight?"

"Of course," he said, offering her a wide smile. "The resort is a sponsor of the event, so I'll be there in an official capacity. I'm in charge of delivering the crown for the pageant. Very important stuff, yes?"

A hint of disappointment washed through her, like it was the high school prom and the boy she'd wanted to ask her couldn't go. It was ridiculous. She was working too. It's not like they could go together.

"Will you save me a dance?" he asked, seeming to read her thoughts.

Kate felt the heat rise in her cheeks. "I'd be honored."

"*C'est magnifique*. I look forward to it," he said, as he backed away from her toward his post, with his hands in his pockets.

THE COMMUNITY CENTER WAS teeming with people there for the ball and to see the culmination of the village royalty pageant. Kate located the table reserved for Mrs. Hall's party and made her way back to where Mrs. Hall and Jake waited.

"Cynthia!" An attractive blonde woman approached out of the sea of people and air-kissed Mrs. Hall's cheeks in greeting. "Is this where you've been keeping yourself the last few days. Such a quaint little village. I love it!"

As Kate got closer, she recognized Tori Van Nuys, one of Mrs. Hall's perceived rivals in the fashion industry.

"Tori, so glad you could get away for a holiday this year, I know how busy you are. I feel like I haven't seen you in weeks."

From vantage point of the average observer, it would seem the two women were old friends, but Kate knew how much Mrs. Hall despised Tori Van Nuys. They had been rivals since their modeling days, and the competition between the two design moguls was often fierce.

"Is this one of your latest creations?" Tori Van Nuys asked, appraising the gown Mrs. Hall wore.

It was a beautiful gown with an ivory sheer over a cranberry A-line cut silk. Kate had admired that design when it first came across Mrs. Hall's desk six months ago. It wasn't a Cynthia Skye-Adams personal design, but it was done by one of her contracted designers.

"Yes. It will be released in my holiday line for next year. Don't you love it?"

To be honest, Tori Van Nuys did look a tad envious from where Kate stood. And with good reason.

"And who are you wearing tonight?" Mrs. Hall asked. The sarcastic tilt of her smile wasn't lost on Tori Van Nuys, who responded with well-veiled disdain.

"Don't you recognize it, darling? This is the design that was on the cover of *Being Beautiful* just this month." It was a dart to the target. Kate knew the coveted holiday cover was a sore spot for Mrs. Hall, and Tori Van Nuys had won that one three years in a row.

Mrs. Hall shifted uncomfortably on her feet and a spark of anger flashed in her eyes, but she held her composure well.

"It's lovely. And I applaud your confidence in wearing it."

Ouch.

Kate stepped into place beside Mrs. Hall, distracting Tori Van Nuys from her next verbal assault, while Mrs. Hall smirked like one who'd just drawn first blood.

"Ms. Van Nuys, it's lovely to see you. Your gown is gorgeous as usual."

"Kate, you are always so sweet. And your gown is divine. Another Skye-Adams original?"

Kate nodded. The gown Paige had sent over was one of Kate's favorites. A stunning strapless forest green mermaid cut with perfectly fitted bodice covered in mother of pearl beads. Like it had been made just for her.

"Well, I love it anyway," Tori Van Nuys said, patting Kate on the arm. Sweet, but patronizing.

Mrs. Hall and Kate laughed, the proper response for what was supposed to sound like it was meant as a joke but clearly wasn't.

Turning to Mrs. Hall, Kate announced, "Your table is ready, Mrs. Hall."

"Thank you, Kate. It's good to see you, Tori. Let's catch up soon, shall we?"

"I'll have my assistant call Kate."

"You do that."

As they wound through the maze of tables to their

seats near the stage area, Mrs. Hall whispered through gritted teeth, "I can't stand that woman and her *Being Beautiful* cover. She's been absolutely unbearable ever since they did that first feature."

Kate just nodded. No use drawing attention to pesky facts, like how Mrs. Hall would probably be willing to kill for that honor.

When they got to the table, Mrs. Hall stood by her seat waiting for Jake. "My chair, Jake," she said when he sauntered to his place, standing with his hands in his pockets like he didn't know what she expected.

"Sorry, Mother," he said. He held the chair for his mother and then slid into his own seat.

Kate rolled her eyes and took her seat.

The dinner was served in stately affair. Kate recognized several of the waitstaff from the resort. She searched the room for Luca. He had to be around somewhere. He was in charge of the crown, after all.

"Good evening, Mrs. Hall," Luca said, suddenly appearing beside Kate's chair. He nodded to her, and his eyes sparkled with mischief. "Ms. Curtis. How is your dinner tonight?"

"Everything is exquisite, Luca," Mrs. Hall said. "I believe your chef has outdone himself tonight."

"Ah, thank you, madame, I'll bring him your compliments." He glanced briefly over his shoulder at the stage, then said, "Will you excuse me? The festivities are about to begin." He flashed another grin at Kate and her heart skipped a beat. "Ms. Curtis."

She watched him walk away.

"I think our Kate is infatuated with the bellboy, Mother," Jake said, eyeing her suspiciously.

"Here, here, Kate!" Mrs. Hall lifted her champagne flute in salute. "I can't blame you one bit. I know I wouldn't kick him out of the bed." She sipped her champagne.

Kate winced at the pain of that thought.

"Mother, please," Jake whined.

"Oh, don't be a prude, Jake. Being on a diet doesn't mean you can't look at the menu, am I right, Kate?" Mrs. Hall's tongue was getting looser by the minute. How much champagne had she had?

"*Mesdames et Messieurs*, welcome to the Huckleberry Falls community Christmas Eve pageant." Luca stood on the stage, at the microphone. He looked amazing in his tuxedo. "It is my pleasure to introduce our esteemed mayor for the pronouncement of this year's Christmas royalty. Please join me in welcoming the beautiful Mayor Chapman." He held out his arm to the left of the stage where she stood waiting.

"Thank you, Luca," the mayor said after the applause died down. "Isn't he charming?" Several people clapped again, Luca bowed slightly, and moved a couple steps behind the mayor. She turned stage left and said, "And now for your Christmas royal court—"

Kate had been looking forward to this moment.

Phase One in the plan to force Mrs. Hall to recognize her talent as a designer. She knew that Mrs. Hall would be verbally assessing each gown just under her breath as the ladies walked across the stage, the same way she assessed the catwalk during a showcase. She angled her chair closer to Mrs. Hall's, hoping to hear the private dialogue.

One by one, the mayor announced the candidates and their escorts, and one by one, each Christmas princess glided across the stage on the arm of her prince.

Kate listened intently to Mrs. Hall's muttering. *Nice lines. Alluring neckline—perhaps a longer skirt. What was that designer thinking?* At that one, Mrs. Hall shuddered in horror. *Probably a Tori Van Nuys.*

Then the mayor announced, "Princess Cleo Klausse escorted by Mr. Kayne Frost, our reigning Christmas king," and Cleo stepped onto the stage wearing the strapless ice blue gown Kate had designed. Its fitted bodice was made of satin and had beading along the trim and down the folds in the front. At the hips, it flared out in mock coattails, overlaying the tulle that billowed out over a full satin skirt. Kate's crowning glory. It had stolen her breath every time she'd seen it, but tonight, as Cleo drifted carefully along the stage like an elegant angelic cloud, she made the gown appear even more exquisite than Kate remembered. A tear slipped down her cheek.

Gasps ran through the audience, and Kate suddenly realized Mrs. Hall wasn't muttering anymore. She turned to look at her. Mrs. Hall was frowning. A deep furrow creased her perfect brow line, and Kate's heart clamored in her chest in a rhythm not her own.

Mrs. Hall *never* frowned.

"Is everything alright, Mrs. Hall?" Kate asked. Her blood felt frozen in her veins.

Mrs. Hall suddenly leaned toward Kate and said, "So help me, Kate, if that's one of Tori Van Nuys's gowns, I'm going to slit my own throat. Where is that witch?" She craned her neck to find where Tori Van Nuys was sitting, but Tori Van Nuys was frowning too, and craning her neck to look for Mrs. Hall's reaction.

Mrs. Hall settled back into her seat to pretend she was completely at ease. She nodded at the other woman with a satisfied smirk on her face.

"Kate," Mrs. Hall whispered through the gritted teeth of her forced grin. "I want to meet that girl immediately after this silly crowning business. Before Tori can think of it."

From the way Tori Van Nuys was squirming in her chair, it was too late for that.

Kate closed her eyes and inhaled a deep breath, then released it slowly, allowing the rhythm of her heart to syncopate. When she opened her eyes, she searched for Luca on stage and found him gazing back at her, eyes gleaming with pride. He nodded, and a broad smile broke over his face.

The rest of the crowning ceremony was a blur. Kate didn't even notice when they announced the king and queen. Her heart was soaring, and the only person she wanted to share this moment with was standing on stage twenty feet away.

The royal court moved to the dance floor to take their first dance and officially start the ball portion of the evening. Mrs. Hall rose beside Kate and nudged her with her elbow, prodding her roughly back to the present.

"I see Tori is angling toward her already, the vulture. Go, Kate!"

Kate cast a last glance toward Luca and pointed to the dancefloor. He nodded. He would meet her there.

As the first dance ended, Kate waved to catch Cleo's eye. Cleo nodded and moved toward her.

"Kate, hi, I'm so glad you could make it," Cleo said a little out of breath. Her eyes were still wide, like she wasn't sure what had happened.

"Cleo, you were so beautiful up there."

The girl dropped her gaze to the floor. "Thank you," she said, then lifted her head again. "I owe you a huge debt, Kate. This dress… I don't even know what to say."

"You made it beautiful, Cleo. Thank you for being willing to wear it."

Mrs. Hall stepped in on Kate's right side. "And who is this young lady, Kate?" She held out her hand in greeting toward Cleo. Something Mrs. Hall rarely did.

"Mrs. Hall—"

Mrs. Hall cleared her throat and shook her head, her way of telling Kate to introduce her professionally.

"Excuse me, Cynthia Skye-Adams, this is Cleo Klausse. Cleo, Cynthia Skye-Adams."

Cleo took Mrs. Hall's hand. "It's nice to meet you."

Cleo had no idea who Cynthia Skye-Adams was. Kate fought the urge to laugh. The disappointment emanating from Mrs. Hall in that moment was almost palpable, but she forced herself to bury it for the sake of the business at hand.

"It's lovely to meet you too. You were absolutely stunning tonight."

"That's exactly what I said to myself," Tori Van Nuys said, suddenly appearing on Kate's left.

Mrs. Hall glared past Kate at the woman encroaching on her territory, then plied a carefully crafted smile and turned back to Cleo.

"Did you design this dress yourself, Cleo?" Mrs. Hall asked.

Cleo looked at Kate with a question in her eyes. Kate wasn't sure how to help her. She felt awful for putting Cleo in this situation.

"No…"

"Well, who is your designer?" Mrs. Hall pressed closer.

"Was it Linda?" asked Tori Van Nuys, closing in from the other side, almost edging Kate out completely.

Cleo looked from one woman to the other, then back to Kate. She seemed utterly overwhelmed and confused. Kate smiled and nodded almost imperceptibly, willing her to say the words.

"It wasn't Linda," Cleo finally said, then lifting a hand toward Kate, she added, "It was Kate."

"Kate who?" demanded Mrs. Hall, barely holding onto her thin semblance of forced sweetness.

But Tori Van Nuys took a step back, and turning to Kate, asked, "You designed this dress, Kate?"

Kate nodded. Her heart was up in her throat. "Yes."

Mrs. Hall fell back as though she'd been slapped, and her gaze traveled between the dress and Kate, once, twice, three times. "Are you certain?" The question was directed at Cleo.

"As sure as I'm wearing it." Cleo grinned at Kate. "I don't know much about fashion, but I do know that Kate is a genius at it."

One of the men from the royal court approached Cleo from behind and tapped on her shoulder. "Will you dance with me, Cleo?"

Cleo blushed and took his offered hand. "I'll talk to you later, Kate."

Kate watched as Cleo returned to the dance floor.

"I'd love to see your portfolio, Kate." It was Tori Van Nuys. "If your other designs are anything like this, I can find a place for you on my design floor."

"Now just a minute, Kate is my assistant. If anyone is

going to look at her portfolio, it will be me." She turned to Kate. "Bring me your portfolio first thing in the morning."

"You mean you haven't even seen your own assistant's portfolio? That's ridiculous, Cynthia!"

"Don't you tell me what to do with my assistant, Tori!"

A warm hand hooked Kate's arm and coaxed her gently backward. The two women were so entrenched in their argument, they didn't even notice. They just continued whisper-yelling, completely oblivious to the rest of the world around them.

Luca whispered in her ear, "It's a masterpiece, Kate. Nothing you said prepared me for the reality of it. You are an amazing designer..." He twirled her around to face him. Wrapping his left arm around her waist and taking her right hand in his, he swept her onto the dance floor. "...And an even more amazing woman."

"I don't know about that," she said, the heat rising to her cheeks. "But between Tori Van Nuys and Cynthia Skye-Adams, my dream of working on the design floor might actually come true. I feel like the luckiest person alive right now!"

"They're the lucky ones, Kate. Whoever you choose. I believe that."

Their eyes met for a long moment, and the dance floor suddenly felt very crowded.

"Can we maybe get some air?" Kate asked.

Luca nodded and led her out to the terrace overlooking the back lawn. It was snowing, and the twinkling Christmas lights reflected off the fresh powder blanketing the ground.

"It's so beautiful," said Kate, staring out over the garden "I'll be sorry to leave."

"I wish you didn't have to," Luca said. His gaze bore into hers. "I know I can't ask you to stay, so I won't, but I do hope you know that you could… if you wanted to."

Kate turned to face him. It wasn't as simple as that. She might *want* to stay, but if she was finally getting her shot at designing, and she gave it up before it even started, she would never forgive herself. The cold wind chilled her bare arms, and she trembled.

"Are you cold?" Luca slipped his jacket off and draped it over her shoulders, wrapping it tightly around her. "We can go back inside if you like." He kept his eyes on hers, expectantly.

"I just… I have to see if I can do this." She pulled his jacket tighter around her. But if she was honest with herself, it wasn't just the wind that was causing her to tremble.

"I know. But you can't blame a guy for wishing."

Kate couldn't be sure in the dim light of the terrace, but she thought there were tears glistening in Luca's eyes. She wanted to make it better.

"Hmm…" she said, glancing around the terrace. "You know what I find strange?"

"What's that?"

"At the carnival they had mistletoe hung up every five feet, but here? Not a twig. You suppose Jake used it all up?"

Luca raised his head to study the rafters of the overhang. "That is odd." His eyes returned to hers, and a broad smile stretched across his lips. "But you are right about one thing."

"Oh yeah?"

"Mm-hm. You *are* the luckiest person alive. Because I just happen…" Luca reached into the pocket of the jacket she had wrapped around her shoulders and withdrew a tiny sprig of mistletoe. "...to have the last bit of mistletoe in the entire state of Wyoming..." He held it up for her inspection. "...right here."

She took it gingerly between her thumb and forefinger, drawing it in for a closer look. "Well, what do you know. And here I thought there was nothing to see in Wyoming." And whether it was the boost of confidence from the success with Cleo's dress, or the champagne she'd had with dinner, Kate couldn't be sure — she raised up on her tiptoes, dangled it over his head, and whispered, "Oh, ho ho, look who's under the mistletoe now."

Luca kissed her then, slowly, working his lips over hers like an artist's brush painting a masterpiece. Her whole body burned under his touch. She wasn't cold anymore, but in that moment, she wished she could freeze time.

CHAPTER TWELVE
See the Flowing Bowl Before Us

O N Christmas Eve morning, when Kate arrived at Mrs. Hall's suite for her daily briefing, Jake answered the door. He wore gray dress slacks and a vest accented by a royal blue shirt and black tie. It was strange that he was in his finery so early in the morning.

"Won't you come in, Kate?" he said with a smile that, for once, held no irony.

Kate frowned. Something was definitely off.

"Would you like to sit down? Mother will be with you shortly." He gestured toward a wingback chair. "In the meantime, would you like some coffee? Perhaps a scone? There's cranberry, blueberry, or raspberry. The pastry chef at this place is superb."

It was the most Jake had ever said to her without

adding an inappropriate innuendo. Kate raised an eyebrow and studied him closely. Maybe Jake had a twin brother she'd never met. Of course, that would make Jake the evil twin.

She shook her head. "No, thank you." She sat down on the edge of the seat. If this was to be an ambush, she didn't want to get too comfortable.

When the door to Mrs. Hall's bedroom burst open, Kate's heart jumped up to her throat, and she stood abruptly, not wanting to be caught sitting on the job.

"Welcome, Kate! I'm so sorry to keep you waiting." Mrs. Hall wore her brightest smile and was dressed in her favorite power suit reserved for high profile meetings. "No, please, sit down, sit down. Did Jake offer you a scone?"

"Yes, he did, thank you." Kate furrowed her brow and cautiously lowered herself back into the chair. It was beginning to feel an awful lot like she was trapped in an episode of the *Twilight Zone*. "I'm sorry, Mrs. Hall, is there a conference call this morning?" She searched the calendar on her phone. "I don't have it on the schedule." Kate winced, awaiting the inevitable tongue-lashing about how inefficient she was.

It never came.

"No, no. Nothing on the schedule this morning. It's Christmas Eve, darling. I'm not Ebenezer Scrooge." She sat on the settee across from Kate and stared at her in expectation.

Kate wasn't sure what she was waiting for. This was usually the moment when she ran through the agenda for the day and gave Kate a list of extra duties longer than her scarf.

"Ordinarily, I'd ask my assistant to contact you and formally request your portfolio." She laughed awkwardly. "But well…" Mrs. Hall gestured toward her with an open hand. "…that won't exactly work in this case."

There was a weighty pause, then Mrs. Hall cleared her throat and leaned forward. "Listen, Kate, I don't want you to talk to Tori Van Nuys until you and I have had a chance to discuss your future. Will you do that for me?"

Now the twilight zone made sense—Jake on his best behavior, Mrs. Hall's power suit… *scones*, for crying out loud.

"Mrs. Hall, I'm so sorry. Ms. Van Nuys sent a messenger for my portfolio an hour ago. I didn't realize… I'm sorry."

Mrs. Hall inhaled sharply, but quickly recovered her sweet façade. "I see. Well, I can't say that I blame you, Kate. To be quite honest, if I were Tori, I would have done the exact same thing. She's a shrewd woman." She leaned back against her seat once again, no doubt wanting to appear nonchalant about the whole matter. She didn't realize that Kate knew all her body language. She'd been reading it for five years. Inside, the woman was throwing fits.

"I'll tell you what, Kate. I've been thinking about this for some time now, and I am prepared to offer you a sizable contract to stay on with me." She waved her hand dismissively, like the whole thing was of no consequence to her.

"On the design floor?"

"We can discuss the terms later." She stood and walked to the desk, scribbled something on the notepad there, ripped off the page, and handed it to Kate.

Kate looked at it and froze.

It was an astonishing figure.

"I know this is a lot at once, so I want you to take some time to think about it. Call your family. Enjoy the party tonight and your holiday tomorrow. You can give me your answer when we get back to New York."

"Thank you, Mrs. Hall. That's more than generous." Kate stood and walked to the door.

"Kate…" Mrs. Hall followed close behind her. "You're very talented." She wore her signature angelic smile as she opened the door to see Kate out.

Once in the hall with the door closed behind her, Kate texted Luca.

ME: YOU'RE NEVER GONNA BELIEVE WHAT JUST HAPPENED.

KATE ADMIRED HER REFLECTION in the mirror. There was no use in letting the gown go to waste, and since Mrs. Hall had given Kate the evening off to celebrate Christmas Eve as she saw fit, she saw fit to attend the resort's traditional Christmas Eve dinner party in the gown she had designed for Mrs. Hall.

Mrs. Stradley had been able to do some last-minute alterations for her, and it was a perfect fit.

There was a knock on her door, and Kate took one last look before she turned to open it.

"Hi." Seeing Luca in his tuxedo with the gold tie and vest, matched perfectly to her gown, made Kate's breath catch in her throat.

"You look exquisite. Are you ready?" He offered his arm to her as if he were a prince and she were Cinderella. She felt a bit like Cinderella at that — minus the glass slippers. Those would have been a horrifying mistake.

They made their way to the banquet hall where the party was beginning. They were a few minutes late, but Luca had reserved their seats. As they neared the entrance, Luca's phone buzzed.

"I'm sorry, Kate. I have to take this. Resort business." He left her by the door and took a few steps into the corridor to answer it.

Kate waited, admiring the decorations. She was about to round the corner to see what had been done in the banquet room when she heard voices just on the other side of the wall.

"Are you really planning to put her on the design floor?" It was Jake's voice. Kate leaned closer to hear.

"It's clear that she has a spark of talent, but honestly, I can't afford to lose her as an assistant. It takes simply ages to get them just how I want them. Oh, I'll throw her a couple little design jobs here and there, to keep her happy. Nothing that matters too much."

Jake laughed. The sound of it sent a chill down Kate's spine.

"I'll make sure the contract is for her current job but with a clause up front making everything she designs property of the company. That ought to cover us on the off-chance she does something inspired."

"You mean like that gown last night?"

"Exactly. Starting with that gown and everything since. Trust me, Jake. I've seen the starry-eyed dreamers before. They're so happy to get a designing contract, they don't care what the terms are."

Kate felt nauseous.

That two-bit fraud. After all the sweetness and the *don't-talk-to-Tori-until-I-have-my-chance* talk. Kate could feel the pent-up frustration and stress from her job these past few years boiling to the surface, and she knew they were in danger of a very real explosion at any moment. Would it be so bad? Probably. Here in front of all these people.

She closed her eyes, drew in a deep breath, and released it slowly, consciously blowing out the tension with it.

"Everything okay?" Luca asked, returning from his phone call.

"Not really, but I'll be fine. How about you?" She pointed at his phone. "Everything okay?"

"Yes. Just a vendor scheduling thing. Nothing major." Luca slid the phone back into his pocket and held up his arm for her. "Ready?"

"Ready as I'll ever be," she said, hooking her hand around his arm. Kate wished she could be as sure as she sounded.

Arm in arm, Kate and Luca strode into the room. Luca pointed out their table, and they began the walk through the maze of people. The room suddenly grew quieter and the whispers started. Kate wasn't sure what was wrong, but she kept moving. Her grip on Luca's arm tightened.

He leaned close to her ear and whispered, "They like your dress. That's all."

Kate could feel their eyes on her, and she couldn't stop the heat from moving up her neck and into her ears. Luca led her to their seats, where he held her chair while she sat down then took the seat on her left.

There was a string quartet playing *Stille Nacht* in a corner of the room, and in the center of each table was a small fondue pot with a basket of bread cubes and long sticks.

"Fondue?" Luca asked, stabbing a piece of bread with one of the sticks and offering it to Kate.

"Sure." She took the stick from him and dipped it into the pot, coating the bread with the melted cheese.

"Swiss tradition says that if a man drops his bread into the pot, he has to buy a bottle of wine for the table. But if a woman drops hers..." He paused, and there was mischief in his grin.

"What?" she asked. Her hand was suspended above the table, holding the bread precariously over the pot.

"She must kiss the man seated on her left. So, be careful with that... or don't." He waggled his eyebrows.

"That sounds made up," Kate said, carefully drawing her stick of bread back to her plate.

"Of course, it's made up. Brilliant Swiss men made it up to get kisses from pretty girls. The clumsier the better." As if to punctuate his statement, a squeal erupted from a nearby table, and a woman in a blue dress leaned to her left and kissed the man sitting there.

"See?" Luca said. He pointed to the folded cards situated in front of each plate. "All the Christmas Eve traditions are written right there, so there will be no excuses."

"Is that why you sat there?"

"*Bien entendu*—of course."

Kate picked up a card and scanned it. "Hmm... I could really use that bottle of wine though."

Luca stretched across the table, impaling another

chunk of bread on a stick and dipping it in the pot. "Who's to say we can't both get what we want?" He gave it a little shake and the bread plopped into the cheese. "Oops." He lifted his hand and waved, catching the attention of a server, who hurried over to their table.

"Yes, sir?"

"We will need a bottle of wine, George, if you don't mind."

George nodded and hurried toward a table near the wall, fully stocked with bottles of fine wine. He returned directly, uncorked the bottle, and poured them each a small amount, then left the bottle with Luca and rushed away to help another table.

"Your turn," Luca said, nodding toward the fondue pot.

Kate studied Luca for a moment. He was adorable—the twinkle in his eyes, the roguish smile. Who could resist? She grabbed another stick and speared at the bread, then plunged it into the cheese. When she pulled the stick back out, the bread was missing.

"Darn it," she said, shrugging.

Luca inclined his head and raised an eyebrow, shaking his head. "So clumsy, Kate." He crooked a finger at her and pointed at his lips. "Pay up."

Kate leaned into him and pressed her lips to his, lingering much longer than she had intended. The warmth of his kiss spread through her, and she didn't want to stop. Not yet.

The familiar sound of a throat clearing startled her, and she drew back, gazing into Luca's eyes for a long moment. He gestured with his eyes in the direction the sound had come from.

Reluctantly, Kate turned to Mrs. Hall, who stood beside an empty chair on Kate's right. "May we join you, Kate?" she asked. The request was pleasant enough, but the memory of what Kate had overheard only moments before was very raw. Every muscle in Kate's body tensed.

Luca stood briefly while Jake held the chair for his mother. When he sat back down, he slipped his hand onto Kate's under the table and squeezed it. He didn't know what had happened earlier, but he seemed to sense that Kate needed his support.

Mrs. Hall angled toward Kate, and making no pretense, she let her gaze run the full length of Kate's gown. By sheer force of habit, Kate held her breath, hoping Mrs. Hall would approve, but instead of appreciation in her eyes, Kate saw resentment.

"What is *this*?" She gestured toward the gown. "A gift from Tori, I suppose? She's trying to manipulate you with extravagant gifts, Kate. Tell me you're intelligent enough to see through her superficial schemes."

Kate felt the last shred of her restraint stretch to the breaking point, and she made a desperate attempt to maintain control.

"Mrs. Hall, *I* designed this dress. It's the one I had made for you for the Christmas ball." It came out more forceful than she meant it to be.

"What? Well, that's ridiculous, Kate. I've never seen this dress before. I think I would know." There was enough noise coming from the other people in the room, that Mrs. Hall didn't bother to lower her voice either.

"I know you haven't. You refused to look at it." Even louder. People were starting to look at them. "Don't you remember? I believe your exact words were 'Cynthia Skye-

Adams cannot be caught wearing something off the rack of a local shop.' It was your last word on the subject. I remember specifically because you spoke slowly so I. Would. Under. Stand."

Luca released her hand under the table and moved his hand to her shoulder. Was he trying to hold her back?

Mrs. Hall's face began to turn red. Jake leaned toward her and whispered something in her ear. Whatever it was, she glanced around at the tables, and then smiled sweetly and relaxed into her chair.

"Perhaps we can continue this discussion later, Kate."

"That won't be necessary, Mrs. Hall. I've made up my mind about your offer." Kate reached for her clutch. "I am going to have to decline." She opened her purse and pulled the folded letter she had been carrying around with her for the past two years.

"Kate," Mrs. Hall began, "I really think you should take until we get back to New York to think about that. Leave time to negotiate."

Kate slid the folded paper across the table.

"What is this?" Mrs. Hall asked, reaching for the letter.

"My resignation."

"Kate…"

"Thank you, Mrs. Hall, for the valuable learning experience, but I feel like I've reached a point in my employment that I have gleaned all I can from you."

Mrs. Hall stared at her in utter disbelief.

As if on cue, the string quartet began playing *Deck the Halls*.

Kate turned to Luca, who seemed to be hiding his amusement beneath a calm exterior. He held out his hand to her. "Would you like to dance?"

"I would love to."

CHAPTER THIRTEEN
Fast Away the Old Year Passes

"*Joyeux Noël*," Luca said when Kate opened her door on Christmas morning. "I come bearing gifts." He held up a cup of hot coffee. "This is from me, and this…" He handed Kate a manila envelope with her name on it. "…is from Tori Van Nuys."

"Coffee! Oh, thank God!" She grabbed the cup with both hands and let the aroma wash over her, awaking her senses. The thought of the envelope, however, was another matter, and she refused to touch it.

"Um…" Luca quirked an eyebrow and frowned in confusion. "Did you hear me? Tori Van Nuys!" He waved the packet in front of her.

"Yeah, I heard you." She cringed and took it.

"Aren't you going to open it?"

She shuffled to the kitchen counter and dropped the envelope there like it was a hot potato, shaking her head. "I'm afraid. Good news never comes in big envelopes." She sat on a stool and took a sip of her coffee, staring at the envelope like it was loaded with Anthrax.

Luca sat on the other stool and leveled his gaze on her. "What if it's good news?"

That was a trick question, Kate was sure. Because *good* to Luca might mean not getting the job because then there would be no reason for her to return to New York and she could stay there with him. If she were honest with herself, that wouldn't be so bad. Meeting Luca had changed her life. She just wasn't so sure it had changed her dream.

He pushed the envelope toward her. "No use living in fear. Let's find out."

She nodded. Butterflies danced in her stomach. Kate took a deep breath and let it out slowly, lifting the envelope and breaking the seal. She closed her eyes as she reached inside and slid the papers out.

"I can't look," she said, eyes clenched tight. She thrust the stack of papers in Luca's direction.

Gently, he took them from her. She waited in silence, holding her breath.

The silence stretched out much longer than she thought it should. Not a good sign. Suspense began to eat through her carefully constructed composure, so cautiously, she opened one eye to peek at Luca, to study his reaction. His face was void of expression.

No smile. No sadness. Nothing.

Both eyes open wide, she stared at him, staring at her.

"Well, what does it say!?" Kate swatted at Luca's arm.

"'Dear Ms. Curtis, thank you for submitting your

portfolio for review…'" He paused and directed his gaze back at Kate. She wasn't sure if it was for dramatic effect or if he was gauging how heartbroken she would be, but she couldn't wait any longer to find out.

"Oh, my word! Give me that!" She snatched the letter out of his hand and quickly scanned the page. "She loved it." It was barely a whisper. Then her eyes shot to Luca. "She loved it!" Kate leaped off her stool and bounced around the room. "Tori Van Nuys loves my portfolio! She wants to offer me a contract… on the design floor… in New York!"

Luca clapped his hands and laughed. "See? I knew it was good news! You are amazing, and now everyone knows it."

Kate wrapped her arms around him and gazed up into his eyes. He slid his arms around her waist.

"I'm so proud of you," he whispered.

"Thank you." Her heart was full with the realization of her dreams. So why did it seem so bittersweet?

Kate knew the answer. This would be the last time she'd be wrapped up in Luca's arms, and it was a goodbye she didn't want to make.

IT WAS TRUE. LUCA was proud of her, of how she had worked to earn her dreams. It wasn't just dropped in her lap. That made it worth so much more. The fruit of her labors. She was amazing, and she deserved this.

He wouldn't allow himself to be selfish.

But even in his resolution, Kate's excitement seemed to fade when she looked in his eyes. Did he seem sad to her?

"This isn't goodbye, you know. I'll be back, Luca, I promise."

And Luca believed her.

Because that is what his heart wanted to believe.

Luca drove Kate to the airport himself, and they talked the whole way, making plans about how their relationship could work over such a long distance.

As he kissed her goodbye for the last time and climbed into his car for the long drive back alone, he comforted himself with the old adage, *Absence makes the heart grow fonder*. If that were true, he'd be pining for Kate by the time he got back to the resort.

BACK IN NEW YORK, Kate threw herself heart and soul into her new career. Kate quickly found that Tori Van Nuys was an amazing mentor, working closely with Kate as a protégé and guiding her through the world of fashion. Tori was every bit the workaholic Mrs. Hall had been, and Kate knew that the woman's assistant was overworked too. And at times, the fashion industry could be cutthroat, but when one of Kate's designs made the cover of *Being Beautiful* for the first time, Tori threw a party to celebrate her triumph.

But Kate's first thought was to share her success with Luca.

The demands of her schedule were intense though,

and as much as she'd wanted to take a trip out to Huckleberry Falls to see him, she couldn't. So, she called him, but it wasn't the same as being there.

Kate loved what she did. She loved working for Tori and the feeling she got when her designs were on the catwalk in a showcase. But always there was the longing in her soul to be with Luca.

When her first year was almost up, she was called into Tori's office for a meeting.

"As you know, your contract is due for renegotiation this month." Tori indicated the chair across from her. "I just thought we could have a frank discussion about your work and your future."

Kate's stomach flipped. She thought she'd been doing well. Was Tori dissatisfied?

Tori grinned. "Not to worry, Kate, it's a good thing."

The fact that Tori read her so well was one more reason that Kate enjoyed working with her so much. Her sensitivity to the people around her was a novelty, actually. And Kate had noticed over the last year that there was little to no turnover in Tori's studio. Everyone loved her. Even the overworked assistant.

Kate relaxed.

"First, I want to make sure you know that *I* know how talented you are. I have never had a first-year designer win a cover of *Being Beautiful*. In fact, I'm not sure that's ever happened in the history of the magazine. The feature brought a lot of attention to our firm, and with it, I've been hearing a lot of rumblings in the industry of people planning to steal you away from us."

Kate nodded. She had already received several calls from headhunters since the feature had come out.

"Listen, Kate. I'm all about helping people achieve their best success. And I want you to know that wherever your dream takes you, I'll support you. Even if that takes you away from here." Tori reached out and rested her hand on Kate's for a moment. When she released it, she leaned back in her chair and leveled her gaze at Kate. "That being said, I have an offer of my own to keep that from happening." She rose from her seat and went to her desk. She rustled through a stack of paperwork on her desk until she found what she was looking for. Then she tapped the intercom on her phone.

"Lizzie, can you send in our guest?" Tori said into the speaker. Then she returned to her chair. "I did a little digging, Kate, and a lot of work—and trust me when I say, it was hard to keep this a secret from you—but I think I've put together a deal that will make you happy."

Kate felt like she was on pins and needles. She was already happy. The happiest she had ever been in a job her entire life. She was living the dream already.

The door opened and Lizzie entered with a woman right on her heels.

Kate stood in surprise. "Mrs. Stradley?

Mrs. Stradley grinned and pulled Kate in for a warm hug.

"What are you doing here?"

Mrs. Stradley glanced at Tori, who nodded. "Well, I'm here to make a deal."

CHAPTER FOURTEEN
Hail the New Year, Lads and Lasses

IT HAD BEEN ALMOST A WEEK since Kate had called. Of course, she had texted a few times, but the renegotiations of her contract had been taking a lot of her time, and it was only going to get worse once the preparations for the next fashion season began.

In the year since they had met, Kate's dream career had taken off. Luca was proud of her—of her success—but she had only been able to visit a handful of times. And her travel to Europe the past few months had kept her away for longer periods at a time.

Luca missed Kate.

Fortunately, the preparations for the Edelweiss New Year's Eve party had kept him occupied enough that he hadn't been able to dwell on how much he missed her—

how much he wished she could have been here for Christmas—and on the fact that he hadn't heard from her recently, which accounted for his foul mood when the elevator door slid open to the lobby.

"Good morning, Renate," he grunted. "Any messages?"

Renate smiled brightly. She had been trying to cheer him up for the last several days, and he made an effort to oblige her, but it was no use. Especially not today.

"There's a new shop opening in the village," she said.

"Oh? That's nice." Luca pulled the mail out of the tray and sorted through it. He didn't care about a new shop. He didn't care about *any* shop.

"The owner wants to meet with you to discuss some cross-promotion ideas."

"It seems like that would be a conversation to have with the resort's owner, not a manager."

"Oh. Probably. I didn't think of that when she made the appointment."

"She made an appointment?" It came out rougher than he had intended, but he made no apology.

"Yes." Renate winced as if Luca appeared that he might come unglued at any moment. "You were talking to the chef about the party, and it happened so fast. I'm sorry."

Luca exhaled in resignation. "It's okay, Renate. We'll just call her and reschedule a meeting with Gretchen for next week."

Renate bit her lip and frowned. "Um..." Her eyes darted to the manager's office door and back to Luca.

"Oh no... Don't tell me she's here *now*." His shoulders slumped in frustration. "Renate, I don't have time today, the party… and Gretchen's not even here. Why didn't you tell me about this appointment yesterday?"

Renate shrugged. "I'm sorry, Luca. If it helps, the new shop seems like it'll offer some amazing new services for our guests. Can't you just meet with her? Might put you in a better mood. Besides, it couldn't hurt to be the one bringing the information to Gretchen, right?"

"I'll meet with her because she's already here, but we aren't through talking about this." He pointed a finger of warning toward Renate. Luca didn't relish dealing with the kind of people that pandered to the same clientele the resort had. They were often just as difficult as the people they served, especially when they came to Huckleberry Falls from out of state.

Clearly, Luca was going to need a holiday after the holidays were over. Maybe a trip to New York.

He trudged toward the door.

"Luca?" Renate said, drawing his attention just as his hand grasped the doorknob.

"What?"

"Smile." A bright grin spread across her lips as if she was showing him what it should look like.

He shot her a mocking smirk, turned the knob, and stepped into his office. The woman was in a chair with her back to him.

"I'm sorry to keep you waiting, mademoiselle," he said, as he moved to the other side of the desk, focused on the stack of mail in his hands. "Renate tells me you're opening a new shop in the village and you wish to discuss cross-promotion with the resort. Is that right?" When she didn't answer, he glanced up and his heart came skidding to a stop.

"Kate?" It came out as a squeak, and for a moment he was frozen where he stood.

"Hi." She gazed up at him and her emerald eyes twinkled, like she was something straight out of his dreams.

"Kate!" Suddenly he was on the other side of the desk pulling her into his arms, and he wasn't sure if he had leaped the desk in a single bound or if he taken one step at a time like a civilized person. It didn't matter. Kate was there. In Huckleberry Falls. He crushed his lips to hers, like a starving man finding food in the wilderness.

Her hands slid around his neck and her fingers wove through his hair, and it seemed to Luca that she had been starving too.

Luca didn't know how long they held each other. Time seemed to stand still. He wanted to stay in that moment forever.

When Kate broke the seal of their kiss, breathless, Luca found his way back to his senses.

"But how—? Why—? How did you get here?"

"The usual way… three flights, a two-hour train ride, a twenty-minute shuttle, and here I am." She rubbed at the side of his mouth with her thumb as if wiping off a smudge of wayward lipstick. "Actually, it was the strangest thing. I was in the middle of renegotiating my contract with Tori when I suddenly realized I didn't want to be in New York anymore."

Luca felt sick to his stomach. "Kate, that has been your dream forever. And you were doing so well. How—I don't understand—how could you give it up?"

"I didn't give up my dream, Luca. I made it better." She rested her hands on his chest and gazed up at him.

"You are looking at the new owner of *Le Bisou* Boutique. Well, co-owner. Mrs. Stradley and I are partners."

"*Le Bisou*. The Kiss. I like the sound of that. So, if you and Mrs. Stradley are partners, what does that make you and me?" he asked, pulling her closer.

"Happy," she said, wrapping her arms around his neck and stretching up on her tiptoes to kiss him again.

ABOUT THE AUTHOR

LEAH SANDERS is a *USA Today* bestselling author and the middle child in a family of seven children. As a true middle child, she went from high school in Alaska to college in Florida, where she earned a bachelor's degree in secondary education from Southeastern University. She also holds a master's degree in educational technology from Boise State University. She makes her home in Idaho with her husband and four children and teaches high school English.

BOOKS BY LEAH SANDERS

Waltzing with the Wallflower Trilogy
Waltzing with the Wallflower
Beguiling Bridget
Taming Wilde

Two Turtledoves

Sacred Ring

All We See or Seem

Discord

The Parting Gift

The Trouble with Frogs

Deck the Halls